Lucas Malet

The Wages of Sin

Vol. III

Lucas Malet

The Wages of Sin
Vol. III

ISBN/EAN: 9783337065010

Printed in Europe, USA, Canada, Australia, Japan

Cover: Foto ©Andreas Hilbeck / pixelio.de

More available books at **www.hansebooks.com**

THE WAGES OF SIN

A NOVEL

BY

LUCAS MALET

Author of ' Col. Enderby's Wife,' ' A Counsel of Perfection,' etc.

'Did we think victory great ?
'So it is.—But now it seems to me, when it cannot be
 helped, that defeat is great,
'And that death and dismay are great.'

VOLUME III.

London :
SWAN SONNENSCHEIN AND CO.
PATERNOSTER SQUARE
1891

CONTENTS.

BOOK V.—TWO IDYLLS.

CHAPTER V.

LEFT alone Mary Crookenden fell into a considerable meditation, the immediate effect of which was that she went across the sunny pasture, through the plantation into the ugly whitewashed rectory (for all the world just like the house a child draws on a slate) and up to her bedroom. There, from an inner pocket of her travelling bag, she extracted a flattish oblong box of old Dutch silver. Armed with this, and having ascertained that the Rector was still out in the parish and not likely to be back till near dinner time, she sallied forth again ; made her way down into the deer-park, crossed the stream and turned up the grass path which, after passing across the hillside, showing like a winding ribbon of green amid the darker tones of the heath and gorse, dips over the shoulder of the hill to Red Rock Mouth.

She walked slowly, as was indeed only seemly, for she was about attending a funeral. The oblong silver box was, in point of fact, a coffin, containing a body symbolizing much. But whether that body was already a corpse or not Mary was not quite certain. Yet uncertainty only

made her more anxious to complete the obsequies ; for it
appeared to her if a measure of life were still left in it,
burial, deep, uncompromising, final, was even more necessary than if it was already well dead.

The subtleties of the feminine mind are infinite, its
capacities of playing hide-and-seek with its own motives
and desires not to be gauged. Yet even in the case of
that most complex development of female humanity, the
modern young woman, there is, more often than not, an
underlying simplicity and, when it comes to a push, an
innate rectitude with which the casual male observer would
certainly not credit her. She has suspiciously liberal and
cynical fashions of speech, as she has, too frequently,
suspiciously loud and dashing fashions of dress; but
beneath these are a pure mind and fair well-favoured body,
singularly unspoiled and undistorted by the cut of the
garments in which the taste of the hour has impelled her
to clothe them.

And it was precisely this abiding simplicity and inward
rectitude which prompted Mary to set forth now, and do
her best to bury that little corpse (as she trusted) and all
which it symbolized. Upon good resolutions it is sadly
easy to go back, especially for a young lady proverbially
prone to change her mind. But upon an outward act,
however quaintly parabolic, it is not so easy to go back.
Shave your head when you swear, and you are much more
likely to keep your oath, be sure, than if, trusting to the

compelling power of your own high sense of honour merely, you remain unshaven.

So far Mary had regarded her lover, Cyprian Aldham, from the negative rather than the positive standpoint. Had thought less of the positive consequences of her engagement to him, his claims upon her, than of certain not inconceivable developments, from which she believed that engagement would deliver her. But in their late conversation Aldham had ranged the positive consequences very clearly before her. Not what his relation to her enabled her to avoid, but what it made incumbent upon her to undertake—the thought of obligations rather than safeguards—these began to impress Mary Crookenden. And to fulfil those obligations conscientiously, it appeared to her she was called upon to make a very clean sweep of some interesting episodes of the past.

And so, about half way across the pleasant open hill-side, the great network of wooded valleys lying below, carrying the little silver coffin, or shrine—which was it ?— Mary left the grass path, and went up over the heather to the edge of the cliff. There she sat down, on a mossy spot amid the heath, threw aside her hat, and paused, watching.

Along the extreme verge, just here, grow some leggy tufted furzes; their stems for ever shaken by the draught sucking up the cliff face from the beach, nearly three hundred feet below. Their rounded heads are clipt as close by the wind as by any pruning-hook, still they flower. They were now packed thick and close, a blaze of rich yellow blossom scenting the air with that luscious yet cleanly sweetness which seems compact of summer and sunshine and fruitful warmth. Mary sitting there saw, framed and crossed by their pale, polished, many-eyed stems and masses of bloom, the vast plain of water—translucent green here in shore, growing bluer, more opaque and solid for every added hundred yards of distance. The mist had risen, and immediately opposite Tabery Point and the land on the far side of the bay lay along the horizon, in shape like a huge lilac crocodile, out-stretched head and wavy knotted crest, floating asleep upon the confines of that turquoise sea. Rounding the point, a mere black dot amid the blueness, an outward-bound ocean steamer; the smoke from its funnel rising in a tall upright column, and then, caught by some stronger cur-rent in the upper air, trailing back and back horizontally in long fine wisps across miles of sky. The tinkling treble of the streams came faintly from the valleys behind; the deeper note of the waves, breaking slowly, singly, along the coast reached her in rising and falling cadence from the beach beneath; and, deeper note still, the cease-less sullen beat of surf on the far-away bar at the head of the bay. The jackdaws still chattered, the cuckoo called.

For a while Mary watched and listened. Here was fit place for the performance of funeral rites, calling the serene and ample peace of sea and sky to witness that they were duly performed—that she, rooting out of her heart all thought of any other lover, gave herself wholly, without compromise or reservation, to the man whose wife she had promised to be. And the intention was unquestionably a right and pure one, under whatever fantastic garment of outward ceremony she might elect to clothe it.' The intention, yes—but the event? Ah! the event, dear reader, in Mary's case, as in yours and my own, was determined ages ago, written in the stars. Destiny—which is but a poetical name for the great chains of inevitable cause and effect which link indissolubly the whole course of human history—Destiny shapes the event, and so for it we are rarely responsible. All, I think, that is asked of us is, that our effort be towards the best we know or can picture on the narrow lines between the shackling chains —the very narrow lines whereon we are granted to show what spirit we are of by exercise of free will.

And so Mary, carrying out her quaint parable in action, untied the ribbon binding the silver box and raised the lid. Within lay the halves of the broken china monster, benignly grinning dog Toh, symbolizing much. She contemplated him musingly, and that which he symbolized arose and cried to her. The handsome hands that had broken him in two, right across his sacred middle; Colthurst's hour of weakness and misery; Colthurst's strange passion of what he had himself prayed might

prove but hopeless love; Colthurst's genius, the fierce,
lurid rush and glamour of it; Colthurst's dominating
vitality, the current of which had seemed, at moments, to
flow out from him and pass into her, awakening, inspiring
her, soliciting, almost compelling her to sail forth, even as
the outward-bound steamer there, with its far-trailing
smoke-wreaths was sailing forth into the wonder, and
freedom, and delight, and swift-sweeping danger of the
limitless ocean.　And, as she thought of all this—her eyes
fixed on the smoke-wreaths, lengthening and still lengthening as the vessel sped further and further from the sleeping lilac land into the open west—the nostalgia of which
Colthurst had once spoken to her, that terrible ache of
home-sickness for the essence of all that earth, all that
nature, all that art, all that the strong working of man's
spirit in the throes and languor of love have to give,
encircled and possessed, and, in a sense, dissolved Mary
Crookenden.　She knew what it is to have the heart
poured out like water by an agony of longing—longing
undefinable, yet all-embracing, longing, as it seems, for
recovery of a good once ours, lost we know not where or
when, but lost, alas! lost.　And so the girl flung herself
face downwards in the heather, now in the fulness of her
womanhood as in her childhood years ago, with an out
burst of passionate weeping; while the sunshine kissed her
golden head, and the soft breeze whispered around her,
and the tough-stemmed furzes along the cliff edge, that

have valiantly braved the tempest of so many winters, shuddered with small dry rustlings and tickings of pity, as one might suppose, at sight of this tempest of human grief.

There are several stages in a real big cry, as every woman knows. Mary passed through them all. First she cried from that desperation of indefinable longing. As second stage she cried herself very lonely, ill-used, desolate, without a friend in the world; then cried herself tired; cried herself dull and indifferent; finally cried herself a trifle ashamed, poor child.

It was in this last stage that she raised herself, kneeling in the heath, tied the ribbon round the box again, not without a movement of petulant anger towards the benignly grinning monster within and all that he symbolized, leaned over the cliff-edge, clasping a furze stem for safety's sake in her left hand, and threw Toh and his silver coffin over and down.

The tide was nearly high. Single waves broke lazily, creaming up, one by one, in among the purple-gray boulders. The silver box, a point of white light, turned and spun in the air in falling; dropped into the smooth green back of an in-rolling wave, with a flop just audible to the girl watching from the cliff top far above.

Mary rose immediately to her feet. That was done. She had cast away all that James Colthurst had been or come near being to her. Cast away, too, her artistic

aspirations, aspirations after independence and emancipation.   With Bohemia and all that term may stand to
cover—its splendid efforts after the ideal, its bitter, even
sordid experiences of the real, its fiery thoughts, its great
swelling words, its obvious lapses of taste, its uncertain
levels in matters social, its reckless extravagance of emotion, its heroically perpetual, pathetically futile race after
the fabled pot of gold which stands at the base of that
lovely, delusive rainbow we call romance—with all this
she would have nothing more to do.   She had buried all
this in the sea ; bade the blue-green water hide it away
under sand, and seaweed, and rounded boulders ; wash
·out the very remembrance of it.   Henceforward the cultivated well-bred gentleman to whom she had plighted her
troth, his interests, his occupations, his tastes, his home—
that fine old place in Midlandshire—society—the thousand
and one daily duties which wealth and an influential
position bring along with them—these should fill her time,
her mind and heart.   Mary told herself she had acted
wisely, rightly, done that which was safest for all parties
concerned.

So she wiped her wet eyes, tidied herself up a little,
brushed fragments of moss and twig off her gown, pinned
on her hat ; glancing as she did so at the wide, bright
horse-shoe of the bay, at the buff sand-hills and white
splash of a lighthouse and the tide-river working its way
back among the hills, at the long, lilac line of the opposite

coast, at the thin floating smoke-wreaths still marking the track of the steamer. The steamer itself was unseen. It had sailed out into the dusky rose of the sunset—reflections from which were beginning to tinge all the western sea—down over the edge of the world. And Mary was glad it had disappeared ; for notwithstanding her conviction of the wisdom of her conduct, notwithstanding that she had just buried all wild desires in the flowing tide, the thought of that outward-bound vessel still raised a dangerous lump in her throat.

So to avoid all provocation of further outbursts of feeling, of regret for Might-have-been—that cruel, haunting phantom who, to so many of us, so sadly mars all that Is—she set her face homewards, trying hard to think of something very much else—tried to think for instance of Mrs. Crookenden's house-party.

Every one would be arriving just about now. It must be very nearly seven o'clock—the hour one always arrives at Brattleworthy, leaving Waterloo by the eleven o'clock train. Lady Alicia and Violet had come on Wednesday ; but Mr. Winterbotham was unable to get away till the end of the week. He and Mr. Duckingfield—sometime an Indian Commissioner, now member for the Yeomouth Division, a widower, supposed not to be unwilling to make another matrimonial venture in the solid and amiable form of Adela Crookenden ;—Mrs. Carmichael and her second daughter ; Mr. Evershed, a clerk in the Foreign Office ; and little Freddy

Hellard, one of Lord Combmartin's younger sons on leave from Sandhurst, were all coming this evening in company with Lancelot.   Tiresome people !   Mary wished them anywhere.   It was so disagreeable to face them all now just in the first blush of her engagement.   People are so stupid and curious when you're just engaged.   They have a way of staring at you to see where the change comes in.   However, to-morrow she had promised Cyprian to go over to Beera, and spend Easter Sunday with him.   It would be rather nice, at all events as enabling her to escape curious eyes.   On Monday she must encounter them all, for the Rector had promised to dine at Slerracombe House.   And when would she see Lancelot ?   Mary felt a wee bit aggrieved by Lancelot.   She had written him really the very nicest of notes announcing her engagement ; telling him it would never make any difference, that he always would be, as he always had been, the very dearest of cousins—and he had not answered it.   It was vexatious of him not to have written.   Having heard from him and got that over would have made meeting him much easier, much less awkward.

Mary's thoughts lingered round Lancelot, as she went slowly down over the sunny heath, white scuts twinkling away to right and left, as the rabbits—out for their supper and evening game of play—scurried off into their burrows.   She was tired—tired with helping to decorate Brattle-worthy Church all the morning for to-morrow's festival in company with the two Crookenden girls and the rather irrepressible Violet—tired by her interview with Cyprian Aldham—tired by her walk—tired by her big cry. And this sense of exhaustion, combined with thoughts of Lancelot and the sight of the scurrying rabbits, not unnaturally caused her mind to revert to a certain other big cry in which both her cousin and rabbits had played a part. She paused a few yards short of the grass path.

How funny, it must all have taken place almost exactly here! At sunset, too, when the shadows were long, slanting, as her own shadow slanted now, right across the hillside to the clump of wind-clipt oaks on the left. There were people singing, she remembered; men from Beera Mills and young girls. And then there was the couple who followed them—the painter whom Lance had prevented her speaking to. Lance had always held the same views on that point, had always looked askance at her artistic proclivities. Well, he might be easy on that score now, anyhow, for her artistic proclivities had gone into the sea in dog Toh's silver coffin.

Mary sighed; the lump rose again in her throat.

She must think of something else.

The artist had a young woman with him who had spoken of her, Mary's, 'black nurse.' In reply he had said (how oddly it all came back to her!) 'black nurse? That's most suitably picturesque.'—He had on a check shooting jacket.

Really it was very strange that she should remember

the little episode so distinctly!—Mary was quite amused
at the precision of her own vision as she reconstructed the
scene bit by bit.

Lance had called him a cad, and—and in speaking he
stammered.

Mary gave a cry as her thought passed, in an instant,
from idle musing to amazed comprehension.—The young
woman had worn a grey gown.   She was the woman of
Colthurst's ' Road to Ruin.'   The woman of the famous
laughing, fearing, fateful, desperate face, whom all London
had crowded to see.   And the painter—her companion, the
man to whom she beckoned, as he leaned, weary yet strong,
fierce even, upon the broken rotting gate—was James
Colthurst himself.

A sort of panic seized Mary Crookenden.   The sea had
given up its dead with treacherous promptitude.   Refused
burial to that which she so earnestly desired to bury.
Sent it back to confront her, to perplex her, to put hard
questions to her uncommonly difficult of solution.

Had Colthurst known all along, or was he as innocent of
a former meeting as she herself had been ?   She recalled
her childish sensations.   Repulsion and then attraction;
and how often these sensations had repeated themselves in
the last few months.—She had run after him along this
very grass path, eager to speak to him.   Did he remember
that ?   Mary's panic had a superstitious touch in it.   For
it seemed to her there was something abnormal and

portentous in the sudden recrudescence of this whole matter of Colthurst just when she had made so determined and honest an effort to put it from her; in the discovery that their acquaintance was of so much older date than she had supposed. That discovery agitated her, made her nervous, scared her.

And then the woman of the 'Road to Ruin'—the beckoning, grey-eyed, tragically-laughing woman, the woman whom here, years ago, she had actually seen in the flesh—what of her? Was she dead or living? And, if living, in what relation did she stand to James Colthurst now?

For a moment a spirit of jealousy, sharp-toothed and keen, invaded Mary Crookenden. But it was only for a moment. The girl's pride, and the innate rectitude of which we have already spoken, rose in arms against the invader, refusing it lodging and entertainment, sternly drove it out. Which was more noble than wise on the part of Miss Crookenden. For when nature speaks, even by the voice of a base unlovely passion, it is best carefully to weigh what she says. Her little remarks are very pregnant, and a summary silencing of them frequently ends by landing both yourself and others in an uncommonly tight place.

The Easter moon, large, semi-transparent, irresolute-looking, was just clearing the tops of the trees in the rectory plantation as Mary let the front gate swing to behind her and came up the oval carriage-sweep towards the house. Kent Crookenden stood on the steps of the porch, his feet a little apart, his thumbs stuck in the arm-holes of his waistcoat.

The Rector had filled out somewhat, otherwise his appearance had changed but little during the lapse of the last ten years. The hot fit of the fever of life, the fit which tells on looks, tells on the general constitution both mental and physical, had been got over early in his case, and his appearance had become stationary, like his thoughts, his purposes, his desires. The steady kindness of his eyes still corrected the caustic, half-contemptuous set of his thin-lipped mouth and heavy jaw. But now, as he stood watching the tall, white figure of the young girl coming languidly towards him across the heart-shaped grass-plot between the dusky rose of the dying sunset and growing silver of that large irresolute moon, there was no trace of mockery in the expression of his strongly-marked face, rather a tenderness trenching on compassion, on regret.

' Well, Miss Polly,' he said, as Mary came within speak-ing distance, ' I had nearly given you up for lost. Looked everywhere for you here at home, and then went down to the House, where I fell into the hands of all manner of newly-arrived Philistines, male and female, whom your Aunt˙ Caroline has collected to celebrate this church festival with her ; but no one could tell me of your whereabouts. What have you been doing with yourself, eh, young lady ? '

'I have been away in the deer-park seeing—seeing little ghosts, Uncle Kent,' Mary answered, smiling.

'Then you have been engaged in a most unprofitable business—a business with which young people of your age should have nothing to do.'

'We live pretty fast now,' she said, looking up and still smiling. 'We go into business pretty early now, even into the unprofitable business of ghost-seeing.'

The Rector came down the steps and stood beside the girl on the grey gravel of the carriage-sweep. His under jaw protruded rather ominously, and he questioned her upturned face shrewdly with his steady, kindly eyes.

'Polly, Polly, you have been crying. I can't have you cry, my dear, unless there is very good cause for it ; and then you must tell me, and I will do my best to remove the cause.'

Mary shook her head, and laughed a little.

'I have only been crying for the ghosts,' she said. 'And you can't remove them, Uncle Kent, they are too intangible. They would slip through your fingers. They do through mine. And they don't really matter,' she added, 'not a bit. It is idiotic to fuss about them. Things in general are very good to me. I have all I could ask just now ; all, and a great deal more, than I deserve. And so I must needs go and cry for nothing. For the ghosts are ghosts of nothing, Uncle Kent, of unrealities, of what never has been, never could be.'

Mary shook her head, with a charming air of repudiation.
'I wouldn't have them, Uncle Kent,' she said; 'no, not
at any price.   But I tell you what I will have if you'll let
me—that's the carriage to go over to Beera in time for
morning service to-morrow.   I don't care very much
about braving Aunt Caroline's crowd and seeing each
member of it casting about for an appropriate congratulatory speech with which to greet me.   Cyprian asked me
to go, and I should be glad to go—very glad, if you didn't
mind my taking out one of the horses on Sunday.'

The Rector's eyes still rested questioningly upon her.

'Is Aldham priest enough to lay the ghosts, Polly?' he
asked.

'Yes, I think so.   I feel pretty sure he is,' she answered,
sweetly, gravely.

'Then you are welcome to take every horse in the stable
out on Sunday, my dear.'

CHAPTER VI.

DINNER was over, and the gentlemen had come out of the
dining-room.   The company had sorted itself—rather to
Lancelot's relief—broken up into groups, settled down
for the evening.   Lillie Carmichael was going to sing;
Evershed was turning over her music, choosing a song for
her.   And, as he stood by Lady Alicia Winterbotham's

chair drawn up near the piano, Lancelot took a survey of the rest of his guests. Really he believed every one was very tidily disposed of; only it was a nuisance Freddy Hellard made such an awful noise playing ' Pounce ' with Miss Winterbotham. Lancelot looked at the boy and wondered if he ought not to go and tell him to be quiet. The Rector, Mr. Winterbotham, and Duckingfield with Adela for partner, were well into their first rubber of whist. Adela played a good, dependable game. Lancelot was glad of that, for the three men were first-rate. And it struck him that Adela really looked uncommonly well to-night.—The same thought had occurred to the member for Yeomouth. And as the latter gentleman witnessed the girl's careful judicious play, and saw the set of her fine bust and shapely shoulders above the fan of cards held in her left hand, he arrived at a definite conclusion regarding the state of his affections.

'Yes, I really am very much pleased at my niece's engagement. We all feel the marriage is such a suitable one in every respect. The announcement of it has given general satisfaction. We all feel Mary is extremely fortunate, for Mr. Aldham is so thoroughly nice—so very superior and charming, you know. And he is extremely well-connected. His mother was one of the Northamptonshire Delanys. I should have liked you to meet him; but he is not going out just now—poor Lady Aldham's death—you knew her?'

This from the sofa, just behind Lancelot, in his mother's placid well-bred tones, accompanied by a rattle of the diamond and enamel lockets as the crochet-needle went in and out of the soft white wool.

'Dash it all, Miss Winterbotham, but you know you do cheat like the very—no—no—hold on, look here, it was an eight. It's all right—I swear it was an eight—on a nine. There's the ten—hold on, I say this is real jam,' and the irrepressible Freddy Hellard thump, thumped the cards down on the table with a splendid disregard of every one's ears, nerves, and occupations.

'I am always very pleased to hear of a girl who has been so popular and so much admired as Mary Crookenden making a nice marriage in the end,' Mrs. Carmichael said, in response to her hostess's remarks.

The rattling of the lockets ceased momentarily.— 'I suppose my niece really has been a good deal admired?'

'Unquestionably,' Mrs. Carmichael replied, with the pretty lingering emphasis of her slight Scotch accent.

'Watch it a bit—why, you know you do scratch like anything, Miss Winterbotham; and—five—I'll be shot if it wasn't a five—and that ain't fair, you see, because—ace, two—oh! confound—no, I see, all right—because you know I can't scratch back.'

'Her mother was a good deal admired by some people,' Mrs. Crookenden admitted. 'I can't pretend I ever perceived her great claim to beauty myself, but Mary is extraordinarily like her.'

' Who was she ? '

'Oh ! an American,' Mrs. Crookenden said, much as she might have said an anthropoid ape.

The Slerracombe drawing-room is a big room. Big enough, even when well-lighted as to-night, still to keep corners and spaces of warm shadow through which the backs of the books in their tall cases show as a pleasant well-toned background to the handsome heavy furniture, the plants, screens, tall vases of cut flowers, and to the pretty women, arrayed with that expensiveness and rather lavish revelation of personal charms which characterizes English evening dress. And it was about one of these shadowed corners that Lancelot's eyes lingered while his mother thus complacently discussed and disposed of the question of Mary Crookenden's engagement.

He had had no opportunity of seeing anything of Polly as yet. The duties of hospitality had kept him busy ; and both yesterday and to-day she had been over at Beera. At dinner she sat at his mother's end of the table. Lancelot knew he must speak to her—longed to speak to her—about that same matter of her engagement. Yet dreaded doing so. The goodly youth feared he should make a muddle, and end by saying things best left unsaid. But there she was sitting on the other side of the room alone with Carrie. Perhaps it would be wisest to go and

get it over.   Every one was provided for.   Lady Alicia
was talking to Evershed.

But just as Lancelot set forth, Mrs. Carmichael stopped
him with a question.   He answered it.   Set forth again
only to encounter Violet all dimpling smiles, in a pink
china silk and *mousseline de chiffon* frock which set off her
downy ripeness to perfection.

'Oh! how quite too delightful for words,' she cried.
'You're coming to play "Pounce," Mr. Crookenden?'

Lancelot shook his head.   'No, indeed I'm not,' he
said, good-temperedly.

'Oh, but indeed you are.   I know you are.   Move,
Mr. Hellard.   Make room for your cousin.   Three-handed
"Pounce" is quite the most thrilling game in the whole
world.'

'Yes, come along and play, old chappie,' put in the lively
Freddy.   'You don't look quite fit somehow to-night, and
this festive little gamble as conducted by Miss Winterbotham would brighten you up, dear boy.   'Pon my
honour it would.   Just hold on and try.'

But Lancelot evinced no relish for such brightening up;
he advanced resolutely upon the shadowy corner, a sort
of sinking within him as though he were advancing upon
an enemy's battery, the guns of which might open on him
at any moment.   And so they did open; but it was his
sister Carrie, not Mary, who applied the portfire.

'Oh! Lance, do come and see Polly's engagement

ring,' she exclaimed by way of greeting, holding up her cousin's hand for inspection.

For though Carrie Crookenden was a good girl, kind-hearted and estimable, she did not possess the gift of tact. Indeed if an unfortunate subject was within a conversational mile of her you might be assured she would light upon it with disastrous certainty and despatch. She was a born blunderer. The blunderer, as a rule, while inflicting much misery upon others escapes with a whole skin himself. But it was not so with Carrie Crookenden. For later, at some moment useless alike for avoidance or reparation—usually just as she was getting into bed—she would see what she had done, see it with horrid clearness. Then would lie awake half the night, hot and wretched, in a fever of worry; only to come down to breakfast next morning, the embodiment of solid, buxom, physical well-being, and fall into a precisely parallel error of speech and perception before she had finished her first cup of cream and hot water. For Carrie always drank cream and hot water. Once she had had an attack of heartburn, which so astonished and agitated her that from that celebrated day forward she refused ever to touch tea. But there is a species of heartburn, alas! from which even the most rigorous diet of cream and hot water will not save even the slowest-witted, kindest-hearted, most humble-minded and healthy of maidens; and from an acute attack of that species, Carrie was suffering to-night. Nobody knew anything about it, but Carrie herself. Cyprian Aldham had long appeared to her as a sacred being. She worshipped him—from afar; would have been almost shocked indeed, had he descended from the remote, celestial region in which she supposed him to dwell, and taken any particular notice of her. She was not therefore jealous of her cousin. She acknowledged Mary's superiority to herself in looks, in intelligence in most matters. But the thought of Mary's engagement to the god of her idolatry excited and dazzled what of imagination she had. She looked at her cousin with a touch of awe. Her position and prospects were glorious, unique. And so, lost in wonder, poor Carrie blundered with more than her habitual success to-night; saying to Lancelot—

'Do come and see Polly's engagement ring. Mr. Aldham gave it her to-day. And there's an inscription inside it in Greek, about never parting, you know, never, for ever and ever. The words come round, don't they, Polly, whichever way you read them. I think that's so beautiful, I like it so much, don't you, Lance? May I take it off to show him the inscription?'

Mary was leaning back in the corner of the sofa. Her eyes were half closed. She drew away her hand gently.

'No, you mayn't take it off to show Lance or any one. It must stay where it is, Carrie.'

'For ever and ever?' the girl inquired, with a kind of veiled enthusiasm.

'Oh! yes, I suppose so,' Miss Crookenden said.

Lancelot sat down on the arm of the sofa, just behind his sister; and his sister was exceedingly fond of him in her own quiet, undemonstrative fashion. She derived a great deal of pleasure from his proximity now. It tended to comfort her; though Carrie in her humble simplicity hardly owned she stood in need of comfort. On she blundered.

'For ever and ever—that's so beautiful. I should care for it more than all the pearls outside, though they are so lovely, if I were Polly'—but here the speaker grew hot, fearing she had not been quite delicate, had taken on rather. So, to make matters better, she added—'Wouldn't you, Lance?'—and then hastened to change the subject. 'I was thinking at dinner you'll have to give Polly away, won't you, Lance? Of course Uncle Kent will marry her, and so you stand next. It——'

'Sara Jacobini will give me away. I have settled all about that,' Mary announced, just a trifle quickly.

'Oh! dear, will she? Isn't it rather odd to have a woman give you away? I think Lance would be much nicer.'

Carrie looked reproachfully at her cousin, and rubbed her bare shoulder gently against her brother's coat-sleeve in sign of friendliness. She was hurt for Lance. She did not like him to seem left out in the cold like this.

'It is often done now,' Mary asserted. ' People are continually given away by their mothers, and I am sure Sara has been more than most mothers to me. It is a very reasonable custom.'

' Oh ! well, still I think Lance would be much nicest ! '

Mary could hardly repress a movement of irritation. Really Carrie was ingeniously inconvenient.

But now Miss Carmichael was singing. Her fine mezzo-soprano has a natural tremor in it which is decidedly moving. She had selected a moving song moreover. Gounod's setting of those three short verses by a modern writer in which threefold love—love of lovers, love of nature, love of God—finds as pathetic yet as simple and chastened expression as in any verses, perhaps, in our English tongue.

> ' Oh ! that we two were Maying,
> Over the fragrant leas ;
> Like children with young flowers playing
> Down the stream of the rich spring breeze.'

sang the young voice. And Lancelot, sitting sideways on the arm of the sofa, listened with a certain tightening about the muscles of his throat. And Carrie listened, not venturing in her innate humility to give the words a personal application, but thinking how wonderful and sweet it must be to be Mary Crookenden, such a ring on her finger, and such prospect of sacred companionship ahead. While in Mary herself, thanks to the inherent perversity of things, the song reproduced some touch of the terrible nostalgia she had suffered watching the outward-bound steamer two days ago. Her eyebrows drew together, and her face grew hard. For she believed that nostalgia to be unlawful, a temptation to be resisted and conquered.

· 'Oh! that we two, oh! that we two were Maying'— repeated the young voice.

Is it not, after all, a little too bad to let poetry and sentiment loose on one thus, after dinner, in the well-ordered drawing-room of a country house? The young people present have poetry and sentiment in plenty anyhow, in the mere fact of their youth, sex, and good looks or the reverse—for plainness may afford basis of poetry as well as beauty—without any outside adventitious assistance. And for the rest of us, why, in heaven's name, galvanize into activity just all that which, youth being past, it is so much safer neither to feel nor think of since the future will afford it no legitimate opportunity of exercise? By forty, if we are decent, reputable persons, the limbs of what I may call the body of our affections will be mostly afflicted with paralysis. And it is a gratuitous barbarity to awaken convulsive semblance of life, convulsive jerkings and tinglings, by passing any poetic-emotional electric current through them. Better far let them rest inert and nerveless under whatever covering, reason, philosophy, or even dull-souled custom may have succeeded in spreading over them.

So, anyhow, thought Kent Crookenden, at the whist-table,

when hearing the upsetting words and voice. He lost a trick, indeed, in the effort to repress such involuntary jerkings and tinglings, while he became curiously conscious of the weight of the old miniature which for so many years had hung around his neck. Mr. Duckingfield, too, suffered disturbance of mind and lost not a trick, but sight of his partner's fine bust and amiable countenance above the fan of cards held in her hand—seeing, instead, a grave, far away, beneath the glare of Indian sunlight; the grave of the girl who, as little more than a boy himself, he had loved and won, had watched droop in the fierce heat and had laid to rest beneath the sands of the 'Land of Regrets.' Even the harness of officialism, in which Mr. Winterbotham's timid hopelessly respectable spirit so long had clothed itself, gave a little at the joints. He cleared his throat, fingered his cards, peering through the lights and shadows of the large room at his wife away there by the piano. The music made him uncomfortable, though he never had been, had not a notion how to go 'a-maying.' Possibly Lady Alicia had some notion though, for her small mouth set very close. She tried not to remember a lad in the Guards who had come to Whitney with her brother Shotover the autumn before she married—not to remember a certain luncheon out of doors, on the southern side of one of the great pheasant coverts,—Lord Denier, a former Sir Richard Calmady—the present man's father —a lot of gentlemen were there, and—Lady Alicia went no further along the path of reminiscence, but arranged the *pointe de Venise* frill on her left sleeve. Perceived a little tear in the lace. Really Conyers was not half such a good maid as Dashwood had been. It was annoying of Dashwood's mother to die, and her father to want to have her at home!—Mrs. Carmichael had her thoughts too. Evershed even had his; for the voice was so sadly sweet that he began to wonder if the singer could be troubled by memories, could have ever entertained a fancy for another than his highly desirable self? Such an idea was a little too obviously absurd however; he rejected it with contemptuous incredulity, telling himself he must really be uncommonly far gone if it came to such wonderings as that.

Only Mrs. Crookenden's crochet needle went back and forth unconcernedly through the white wool, while the lockets jangled; and Mr. Freddy Hellard's vernacular broke in, discordant, upon the magic of the song.

'No, why? oh! I say it's too bad to go cavorting around with two kings in that way, Miss Winterbotham.' A series of vigorous thumps on the table, an outburst of very whole-hearted, boyish laughter. 'No, you don't— you bet you don't—not this time, not by a long chalk, Miss Winterbotham.'

Lancelot rested his hands on his sister's plump shoulders.

'Look here, Carrie,' he said. 'I should be no end

grateful to you if you'd go and stop Freddy making that awful row.'

Carrie was not a person of infinite resource. She wanted to please Lancelot, but she also wanted to stay here by him ; her heart warmed under that delightful brotherly caress.

'I don't know how to stop him,' she said.

'Tell him he shall have the monkey he wants if he's a good boy and keeps quiet for the rest of the evening.'

'The monkey—I don't understand.'

'Freddy will, though, fast enough. Stay there a little, do, and keep him quiet.'

Carrie rose reluctantly from her place.

'I'll tell him of course,' she said. 'But I am sure he'd much rather have a bull-dog, and I don't believe they'll let him keep a monkey at Sandhurst, so I'm afraid it will be no good.'

> 'Oh that we two lay sleeping
> Under the churchyard sod ! '

Lancelot slipped off the arm of the sofa into the place just vacated by his sister. He did not wait to hear the end of the verse, fearing the grip on the muscles of his throat might grow a trifle too tight for coherent speech if he did. He crossed his legs. Clasped his hands round one knee. Stared fixedly at the crinkles of an orange and black silk sock around his ankle.

'It's quite true then, Polly,' he said. 'You and Aldham have made it up ? '

Now between the emotional effect of the song, Carrie's blunders, and another feeling, the result of two days spent almost exclusively in Mr. Aldham's company—a feeling which she was anxious not very carefully to analyse— Mary was slightly on edge. It is a fallacy to suppose that suffering breeds sympathy. Very frequently it breeds something of a diametrically opposite kind. A sense of your own ache makes your neighbour's ache appear a trivial affair, an irritating affair, almost an impertinence and intrusion.

'Yes, I wrote and told you so last week.' Mary paused, moved her foot, altering the folds of her skirt. 'I think you might have taken the trouble to answer my letter, Lance,' she said.

'I'm not a great letter-writer, you know,' he replied in the same constrained tone. 'I'm sorry if it was rude of me not to write. But I thought you'd excuse it as we should meet soon, Polly.'

A repressed sputter of laughter from Freddy Hellard, Carrie with largely perplexed countenance, bending over him trying to fathom the joke of her own just repeated doubts as to the rights of pet-keeping likely to be recognized by the military authorities at Sandhurst. And Miss Carmichael's voice, rising into passion in the last words of her song : —

'And our souls at home with God—at home with God.'

Then a hush through the room, a hush more compli-

mentary far than applause, followed by Mr. Winterbotham
clearing his throat with an effect of relief and saying in
his civil, mechanical voice :—'May I trouble you to cut,
Mr. Duckingfield ?—my deal, I believe.' Then general
conversation, by general tacit agreement I suppose not to
let sentiment invade too freely, penetrate too deep.

Mary Crookenden, under cover of that rising hum of
talk, scrutinized the young man nursing his knee, staring
at his black and yellow silk sock. Like many other persons she was slow to learn to accept the consequences of
her own actions. Lancelot was constrained with her ; his
constraint was natural enough under the circumstances,
was, indeed, calculated to save trouble. Mary had much
better have submitted to it. But she could not make up
her mind to submit. She placed her hand on the seat of
the sofa, leaned towards him.

'Lance, dear old boy, haven't you anything more to say
to me than that ?' she asked rather plaintively. 'Say
something nice to me. I can't bear to be at sixes and sevens
with you. Give me your blessing.'—Mary laughed a
little nervously.—'And tell me, Lance, tell me you don't
mind much.'

'I don't see the use of telling lies, exactly—' and there
Lance stopped.

'Oh ! no, of course not ! But promise you won't
detest me for—for it.'

'Don't talk rot, Polly,' he said almost roughly.

That song had made him feel 'awfully badly.' He wished he had stayed over by Lady Alicia.

For a moment Mary debated whether it would not be justifiable and convenient to be angry, intimate he had mislaid his manners, sail away loftily across the room. But she was not particularly happy, and it occurred to her happiness was hardly likely to be increased by quarrelling with so old a friend as Lancelot. She became explanatory.

'Indeed it is best for all of us,' she said. 'I can't go into the ins and outs with you, that is impossible. But, Lance, if I could, if you knew the whole business from beginning to end, I am sure you would see I have done what was wisest, what was right. I was getting into muddles—' Mary hesitated. 'You must take my word for it, Lance, it is best as it is. And so you must try— you will, won't you?—not to mind. Promise to try to forget—and get over it. I shall be miserable if I think you are fretting. Indeed it isn't worth fretting about. Promise to try to get over it, there's a dear, Lance.'

'Oh! I can't promise that.'

Lancelot set his teeth, told himself not to be a selfish fool, saw that Lillie Carmichael was making room for Carrie at the piano—there would be no more songs, then, he was glad of that. Carrie had lessons every year when the family went up to London. She was working her way through Beethoven; each year she added, with much conscientious labour a sonata or two to her re-

pértoire. She plunged now into the last learned. Her playing was ponderously correct, grandly dull. Meanwhile emotion picked up her trailing skirts and fled. Carrie had a fine power of depriving a composer of all pathetic and agitating qualities. Therefore Lancelot found assistance in his sister's performance at this juncture.

'But you know you mustn't bother about me, Polly,' he said presently. 'This is just one of the chances of war. People can't make themselves not care when they do care, any more than they can make themselves care when they don't. All that takes you from the outside, if you know what I mean. You can't avoid it; but it doesn't matter.'

He unclasped his knee, leaned back in the far corner of the sofa, and smiled at his cousin, the tender, sweet-tempered, half amused expression back in his pleasant face.

'I beg your pardon, Polly, I ought to have answered your letter; for it was awfully good of you to write like that, at once, yourself. And Aldham's a splendid fellow' —again Lancelot stopped, the amusement waned somewhat, but he did not lower his eyes.—' He's loads of brains. He'll be able to give you what you want. I am awfully glad you are going to—to marry a man I admire as much as I do him.'

The goodly youth congratulated himself. It seemed to him he was pulling through very fairly well after all.

'I was half afraid you'd got rather into muddles,' he went on. 'I felt that somehow.'

Lancelot crossed his legs again, held his right ankle in his left hand, presenting his cousin with a fine view of a pointed-toed shoe sole.

'And, don't be vexed, Polly, but I couldn't help fancying that beastly old drawing-school went for something in the muddles.'

Mary raised herself from her pretty, pleading, explanatory position, and leaned back in her corner of the sofa.

'Of course it was awfully stupid, but to tell you the truth, I'd got into a horrid fright about that fellow Colthurst. I didn't a bit like your getting so mixed up with him. I'm tremendously glad, all round, you're out of all that.'

Miss Crookenden made an effort to hold her tongue. But the effort was unsuccessful.

'It is too bad,' she said, 'the way all my friends, you and Sara, every one, make such a dead set at Mr. Colthurst.'

'Well, he is a bit of a bounder, you know, Polly,' Lancelot replied, in tones of gentle argument. 'I heard rather a queer story about him in a roundabout way when we were home here at Christmas.'

'What have you heard?' Mary demanded—and then she could have beaten herself for the eagerness of her own voice, the eagerness of her desire to know.

'Oh! well, it was a low sort of story—not the sort of story one cares to repeat unless there's some particular reason for repeating it. If I had seen Madame Jacobini alone that day—the day—you know—we drove together'

—again Lancelot stopped. 'I meant to have spoken to her about it. But as you're quit of the man and his school there's no object in repeating it. I don't see the fun of turning over a muck heap unless one's obliged to. And the man's affairs are no earthly business of mine, now as I say you're quit of him.'

This time Miss Crookenden did succeed in holding her tongue. A silence, therefore, between the two cousins, Carrie pounding away, meanwhile, charging a *rondo* marked *capricioso* in the style of a squadron of heavy dragoons. Suddenly Lancelot asked :—'There aren't two painters of the name of Colthurst, are there, Polly ? '

' Not that I am aware of.'

' Ah ! exactly. He is the one then. I didn't want to do the man an injustice.'

' I say, Lance, all fair and square, *bonâ fide* offer, no deception?' and Freddy Hellard perched on the end of the sofa.

' If you keep quiet,' Lancelot said.

' My dear fellow, I am keeping quiet all I know how— have been all this blessed evening. It was Miss Winterbotham made the row, not me. 'Pon my honour it was. Miss Crookenden, tell him it was—you believe me, don't you ? '

Mary smiled an answer. She was not thinking about Master Freddy. She was putting two and two together, as the saying is ; trying to make them five, fearing that in point of fact they make four. But Freddy was unaware of this. He was usually shy at Miss Crookenden. Her smile mitigated his timidity. He was also extremely jubilant at the prospect of paying his debts, without having recourse to an angry father. He became confidential.

'Between ourselves Miss Winterbotham's frightfully volatile. She is a gay goer, is Miss Winterbotham. You bet, she can make things hum, that girl can. I have been casting an affectionate prophetic eye, Miss Crookenden, over this dear old chappie's future, when he runs in double harness with her and—holy blazes, Lance, what are you up to?'

For Lancelot had caught hold of the boy, whipped him off the end of the sofa, laid him face downwards across his knees, gently but resistlessly pinioned his arms at his sides.

'Don't be an ass, Freddy,' he said.

'But it's perfectly true, Cousin Caroline's been telling —let me up—ask him to let me up, Miss Crookenden ; I shall have a fit in half a minute—telling my respected parents and all the family—ugh—about the double harness for the——'

Lancelot bumped the boy's elbows together behind his back.

'Be quiet, Freddy,' he said.

'But—oh! I say--how can I be quiet when you get bear-fighting like this ? It's a beastly shame. He wants to cut me out of those few dollars, Miss Crookenden. But I'm not covetous. I'll speak the truth at the risk of —stop him, stop him, he's murdering me.—She was just mad, Miss Crookenden, when he wouldn't come and play " Pounce." Her eyes snapped like—ugh—confound it, you are strong, old chap.'

The whist players finished their rubber. A movement at the table, discussion of obscure points of play, counting of gains and losses—then the Rector came over to the sofa. ' Are you ready to go, Polly ? ' he asked.

Mary was more than ready. The evening had not been an altogether successful one. She made her adieux to the company. The Rector and Lancelot followed her into the hall. The distance from the house to the rectory is quite short, and as the night was fine Mary and her uncle proposed walking home. This necessitated a certain amount of wrapping up. Lancelot helped his cousin into the sea-green *cache-misère*, with which the reader is already acquainted, gave her the white lace scarf for her head, hunted under the billiard table, which stands in the centre of the hall, for the pair of overshoes to protect her feet.—They had been kicked some way underneath the table, and Lancelot had to go on all fours to find them. But when found, he did not offer to put them on for her, he let her do that herself; for notwithstanding his solicitude for her comfort, there was an element of reserve in Lancelot's helpfulness to-night when it came to

close quarters. And she barely thanked him. She was
still trying to assure herself two and two may make five,
still seeing four stand uncompromisingly at the foot of the
column. The Rector stood buttoning his overcoat, talking to Lancelot; but Mary paid little heed to their conversation. That story about Colthurst—she wanted to
hear it, wanted not to hear it; wanted, above all, not to
want to hear it. What was Colthurst to her, or she to
Colthurst? As Lancelot said she was quit of the man,
his affairs were no concern of hers; it was foolish, treason-.
able to think of him, and yet—yet—

' I'm going up to town with this young lady to-morrow:
very likely I may not be back before you leave. But if
you think of anything more, estate business, and so forth,
we ought to talk over, send me a line and I will meet you
at Plymouth on my way back. You have quite decided to
sail from there, rather than from Tilbury, have you not? '

' Yes, I think so. You see, it'll give me another day
with my mother; and I'm afraid it will be rather a—well,
a shock to her any way. And Ludovic Quayle joins the
boat at Plymouth, I find.'

Mary looked up from her galosh. It was so tiresome
to put on. The muslin and lace frilling in the hem of her
dress would get into the heel of it.

' Sail? Where are you and Mr. Quayle going, Lance? '
she asked, quickly.

' Oh, well to Bombay first of all, I suppose. I've rather

a fancy for Kashmir and Thibet,' the young man answered
simply and cheerily. 'I should like to have a shot or
two at those jolly big sheep—*oves ammon,* don't you know,
Polly, with the thundering great horns—before the Indian
sportsmen have cleared them all out. And there are
some pretty tidy mountains out there with unpronounce-
able names I should rather like to have a try at.'

Mary let her galosh be, ceased attempting to make two
and two into five. The expression of her fair face was
startled, humbled, looking out from those swathings of
white lace.

'I shall have an awfully interesting time, I expect,'
Lancelot added.

'But, oh Lance, why are you going ?'

The Rector had moved towards the door, which the
footman held open.

'Come along, come along, Miss Polly,' he said. 'Have
a little consideration for a stingy man who has lost
money at cards, and wants to get home to the consolations
of his books and his pipe.'

'Shall you be away long, Lance ? '

'Oh, well, that depends. For as long as Uncle Kent's
willing to take over all my business for me. He's awfully good to me, you know, Polly. A year or two, I
daresay.'

The Rector wished history would not repeat itself.—
'Not that I had the lad's good looks any more than I had

his fortune to offer Mary Coudert,' he thought.—The
little miniature seemed to drag at the black ribbon round
his neck. He went on down the steps.—' Lancelot takes
his misfortune very well,' he said to himself.—' He will
not let it break him as—' the Rector sighed a little as he
stepped out into the broad silver of the moonlight—' as I
let the same misfortune break me.—Polly,' he called
rather huskily, ' Polly, come along, my dear.'

Mary ran down the steps after him, accompanied by
rich rustle of voluminous skirts; and, Cinderella-like,
dropped her slipper—that same but half-adjusted galosh
—in her flight. And the young prince, as in the dear
old story, saw it, picked it up, forestalling the action of
the footman, and strode after her.

' Here, I say, Polly,' he cried. ' Stop half a minute.
You must put this on. It's not safe for you to walk
home in those thin shoes.'

And he knelt down on the loose, shingly gravel of the
carriage drive in front of her.

' There, hold up,' he said cheerily.

Mary could not find anything to say to him just then,
somehow. But she held out her foot—heard the sleepy
grunt of a buck from inside the railings of the deer-park,
the trample of the surf on the bar, the sound of Kent
Crookenden's receding footsteps. Turned to see if he
had gone far, nearly lost her balance in so doing, standing crane-like on one leg. Stretched out her hand to

save herself, found it light on the nearest object capable of affording support—the top of Lancelot's round black head.

Men, even the better bred among them, in their relation to women are divisible into two classes—those who take advantage of such small accidents, slips, misadventures, and those who do not. Lancelot Crookenden belonged to the latter class. For just long enough for the girl to recover her footing the black head remained still, firm as a rock, under her hand. Then the young man sprang up.

'Your shoe's right enough now, Polly,' he said, yet he was very sensible of that tight grip on the muscles of his throat again. 'You mustn't stand about. The wind cuts rather sharp round the corner of the house, though it is such a jolly clear night.'

But Mary had found what to say to him at last. And the words came, with a sense of self-abasement, of self-reproach.

'Lance, you are going away because of me. I have spoilt your home to you—darling old Lance, you must detest me—I have spoilt your life.'

'Oh! not spoilt it, Polly,' he said.

The goodly youth looked very gallant, knightly even notwithstanding the prose of a dress coat and immaculate shirt-front, bare-headed there in the clear chill moonlight.

'Nothing—well, except doing wrong, you know, spoils life, I think.' He stopped a minute—'And I'd rather you married Aldham than anybody, indeed I would. Don't you bother about me. Only, if it wouldn't be a nuisance to you, I should be awfully glad if you would put my name in now and then when you say your prayers. I—well, I think it would help to keep me straight.'

Lancelot thrust his hands into his pockets, whistled even a little as he swung back across the gravel. Away at the head of the bay, between the misty purple of vaguely-seen sea and hills, the lighthouse shone a steady watchful and, as it seemed to the young man, a kindly eye of light.

' "Oh ! that we two "—No, hang the song—'

And he ran up the steps and banged the front door to after him. Violet Winterbotham stood rosy, dimpling, downiest of dormice, ripest of cherries, in the hall.

' Mr. Crookenden, I am simply expiring for a game of billiards,' she said. 'Do come and play with me, will you ? '

' Why, of course, if you like.'

' Oh ! how quite too charming for words.'

Lancelot turned the balls out of a corner pocket.

' I wonder when I'd better tell my mother,' he thought. ' I'm afraid it's rather rough on her. I hope she won't be very much put out.—What will you take, Miss Winterbotham ? Fifteen in fifty—or twenty-five in a hundred,' he said.

CHAPTER VII.

THE first of May came and went, bringing James Colthurst's disciples and admirers assurance that his success
had been no flash in the pan, but that he was fully equal
to sustaining the reputation he had made for himself. For
his work of this year was as strong, as arresting and
complete, as that of last. In one respect, indeed, the
new pictures were, in the estimation of many, superior to
the ' Road to Ruin.' There was less obvious story in
them, and they were not, consequently, open to the charge
of being painted literature, novels on canvas.

The larger one, ' The Chain Harrow,' shows Colthurst's
talent under a fresh aspect, reminding one somewhat, in its
idyllic charm and grace, of Mason. And this without sacrifice of reality. For the lithe, gay-eyed lad hanging on to the
long rope reins to steady the young horse—all foam and
fret—which pulls against the old horse as the two drag the
glistening, jumping links of the great square harrow up
over the rough pasture, is a real lad enough. He belongs
to no fine fanciful age, such as that of which a famous
writer on art so melodiously prophesies, wherein the whirr
of machinery shall be stilled and the steam be relegated
to the housewife's tea-kettle, and toil become a sort of
pious pastime robbed of fatigue, dirt, and all harsh accessories ; an age wherein every one shall be content and as
good as they are pretty. For the sweat stands on his ruddy

face; and the rope reins only do not cut his hands because those hands are much of the texture, as they are
much of the colour, of brick-bats; his leathern leggings
are clogged and sticky with red earth, and the moisture of
the drifting gleaming mist—mist in which the sunshine
hangs as in solution, mist closing in the scene on every
side—drips from the frayed edges of the old sack fastened
by a greasy tag of boot-lace across his shoulders. The
young horse is hot and masterful. The old horse tired.
Neither to them nor to their driver—hardly controlling
the one and urging the other—is the world all beer and
skittles; nor even a world peopled by the charming little
agriculturists and nicely-behaved beasts and birds of Miss
Kate Greenaway's almanacs, or the high-souled devoutly-
reverent-towards-their-betters peasants of Mr. Ruskin's
reconstructed, expurgated edition of the Middle Ages.
The mysterious curse, which gives life (as we know it) at
once its terror and its glory, is on the land, on labour, on
the cattle unwillingly obedient to bit and bridle, on the lad
himself—for all his young masculine vigour—in Colthurst's picture as it has been on all such things from the
dawn of history; as it will be on them—philosophies,
philanthropies, optimistic systems, the English House of
Commons and all its measures even, notwithstanding—
until the end, when the book of earthly existence is
written and closed at last, and the story of our race, its
achievements, its disasters, fully told.

But though the shrewder members of the general public perceived in this picture that which makes all the difference between a great work and a common-place one, it was Colthurst's other and rather smaller painting that attracted most attention, provoked most comment, before which the crowd gathered thickest, wondered most, said least.

A cloudless evening sky—primrose fading upwards into thin crystalline green, and that again into blue—behind the downy greyish buds and crimson, white and flesh-coloured flowers of a row of tall hollyhocks bordering a perspective of narrow garden path. On the right a cottage wall—the whitewash of it discoloured, scaling off in places, defaced by nail-holes, showing the rusty red of the brickwork beneath. And, his back resting against it, sitting on a wooden bench, directly facing the spectator—his knees a little apart, his head poked forward, his loose-lipped mouth slobbering helplessly over the coarse unbleached cloth tied round his neck—a full-grown man, whose dull eyes are majestic in the depth of their pent-up incommunicable sorrow, tenderly nursing an old broken-limbed Dutch doll.

Colthurst, in moments of expansion, was fond of preaching to the young men of the Connop School on the text the power is its own best advocate.

' It is possible so to present things,' he would say, ' that even fops and fribbles think twice before they dare raise a laugh. It all comes back to a question of strength. If you

are strong enough you may go naked and no one will interfere with you. And most certainly, if you are strong enough,
you may present fact without a rag on, and though people
will be scared and try to hide their scare under accusations
of bad taste, and will talk a large amount of long-winded
rubbish about observing the legitimate limits of your art,
they will not venture to smile. They may hate you. But
hate does a man's reputation very little harm. Snap your
fingers at hate. That which stings, that which injures,
because it undermines self-confidence, is ridicule.'

And unquestionably in the case of the idiot, sitting
there among the hollyhocks with the peace of the evening
sky behind him, Colthurst had succeeded in so presenting
his painful subject that criticism of the superior, contemptuous, patronising sort found itself grow somewhat silent
and diffident. The dumb knowledge of degradation, of
alienation from all sweetness of common fellowship
written in the creature's sombre eyes; the instinct of
love, love denied possibility of natural expression, shown
in the clinging action of its monkey-like hands about that
battered wooden idol of a doll, raised the conception to a
plane of tragedy where, as with the fabled head of Medusa,
increase of horror becomes, in a sense, only increase of
beauty.

It is unnecessary to state that Miss Crookenden heard
these two pictures freely discussed during the weeks that
immediately followed her return to London. But it ap-

peared, somehow, that she was always too busy to go and
see them.   Affairs of the trousseau, letters returning
thanks for wedding presents became imperative whenever
Aldham—who spent a good deal of time at his aunt's in
Eccleston Square, at this period, much to that pretty old
lady's happiness—begged her to visit the Academy with
him.   Miss Crookenden appeared to have lost her taste
for picture galleries ; new frocks carried it over the arts
just now.   And this slightly vexed her lover.   He intended
his bride to surprise Midlandshire, and her various new
relations, into admiration by something beyond her personal charms and little air of society.   He was more than
willing that delightful and somewhat exclusive county
should be impressed by his wife's smartness.   But he intended that it should be impressed by her intelligence and
accomplishments as well.   He intended it should fully realise
that he had married a very clever woman.   He thought it
right to set his intentions clearly before her, therefore, one
morning when it struck him the frivolous was gaining
rather reprehensibly over the intellectual.

'I propose that our house shall be a centre of real
culture,' he said to her, in the course of their conversation.
'I should like it to become noted, as certain country
houses one could mention have been and are noted for the
brilliancy of their intellectual atmosphere, for the excellence of the talk you hear and the character of the society
you meet at them.   Few women are more fitted than

yourself, Mary, to be mistress of such a house; and Aldham Revel offers you an excellent *milieu*. To begin with, the house is large enough to hold a considerable number of guests comfortably. The rooms are good, and could be made much more charming at a small expenditure of taste on your part. Poor Lady Aldham's views of decoration were slightly prim and antiquated. Then the library is a really remarkable one. It contains some valuable black-letter books and manuscripts, and a collection of seventeenth and eighteenth century memoirs, which is, I believe, almost unrivalled.'

' I am glad of that,' Mary remarked.

She was occupied in setting out a number of more or less costly offerings on a table in the white and apricot-coloured drawing-room.

' You are fond of memoirs ? ' Aldham asked.

' No, I don't care for them particularly, but Sara Jacobini is devoted to them.'

Mr. Aldham was one of those persons who are rarely guilty of the weakness of an exclamation. But his lips became slightly compressed. It is impossible for two people to entertain a latent dislike of each other without betraying themselves on many small occasions. Aldham had long ago discovered that his *fiancée's* companion had no special devotion towards him. He very naturally, therefore, returned the compliment by being by no means particularly attached to her. Madame Jacobini, moreover, presented a difficulty. Where was she to come in, in the new establishment,? If he could have had his way he would have answered concisely—nowhere. But he foresaw that on this point his opinion and that of Miss Crookenden were not likely to be entirely at one. He therefore deferred the discussion of it to a more convenient season, and returned to the list of attractions supplied by Aldham Revel.

'The pictures will please you, too,' he said. 'My grandfather had a great taste for the English landscape school. He made a very creditable collection of Constables, De Wints, Morlands, and Callcotts. Two of the best "old" Cromes I know hang in the little cedar drawing-room. Remind me to show you them when we go down next week.'

'Yes,' assented Mary.

Aldham remarked that—the visiting of picture galleries excepted—she almost invariably did assent. This pleased him. It was as it should be. Still he could not help noticing a certain listlessness in her tone. To-day he had brought her, on behalf of his uncle, the most costly offering of all—poor Lady Aldham's diamonds, which had been cleaned and in part reset. They glittered and flashed—a couple of necklaces, five stars, some pendants and brooches—as they rested on the purple velvet cushions of their respective cases, really a royal sort of gift for any bride to receive. Aldham glanced from them to their new owner. The woman and the jewels suited each other to admiration. He was genuinely proud of both. But an increasing longing to mould, fashion, in a sense, use the beautiful girl stirred in him. For it is incontestable that the natural man in us survives much disintegrating action of high civilisation; and a pretty strong dash of the sultan remained in this clean-shaven, fine-featured, black-coated young priest. It struck him that Miss Crookenden took both his conversation, his gifts, and the very pleasant position he offered her, a trifle too much for granted—that she seemed insufficiently sensible of the excellence of the marriage she was about to make. This nettled him slightly.

'Suppose, Mary,' he said suddenly, in that clear delicately incisive voice of his, 'suppose you leave off arranging the presents for a little while, and give your mind wholly to our talk. I want to see you interested, genuinely, spontaneously interested in the thought of our future life together.'

'I am interested, profoundly interested,' Miss Crookenden answered. She seemed to deliberate for a few seconds. Then she moved away from the table and its display of glories, sat down near Cyprian Aldham, smiling at him very sweetly. 'Well, go on, plan it all out, give me the stage directions, teach me my part,' she said.

Aldham laughed a little with an irresistible movement of satisfaction.

'You are charmingly submissive, Mary. Will this most commendable and captivating attitude continue?'

'That is my desire,' Mary Crookenden said. And she said it seriously, looking full at her lover.

Would it continue? To Mary that was the most vital of questions just now. She had mentioned to Madame Jacobini six weeks ago as proof of Mr. Aldham's high eligibility that he gave her no feelings. But he had begun giving her feelings. Notably a feeling that there was, to use a hackneyed illustration, a hand of steel within the velvet glove of his fine manner. She began to see through the covering of soft flesh to the bone, the skeleton so to speak of Mr. Aldham's character. She found nothing indefinite, nothing flabby in the constitution of that character. She figured it to herself under the form of some well-proportioned classic building—the parts carefully adjusted, every stone in its place, a sufficient amount of decoration to make it very agreeable to the eye, foundations, too, well planted, sunk deep. It had no secret chambers in it. It stood there orderly, finished, prepared to justify every legitimate demand; presenting itself fearlessly, proudly, arrogantly almost for observation. But it had not grown, it had been made. It was the result of effort, the result of tradition, of circumstance. Every building, unless actually ruinous, is capable of conversion into a prison, if needs be. And the feeling grew on Mary that the handsome building of Cyprian Aldham's character was very capable of conversion into a prison for Cyprian Aldham's wife.   To be happy with him you must conform to his tastes, his wishes, his intentions—how very often, by the way, that phrase 'I intend' was on his lips !   And would she be able to conform and thus secure happiness ? Mary hoped so, hoped so honestly.   She acknowledged to herself she had made a convenience of Aldham's affection for her.   She admitted she was under an obligation to him on that account.   This made her scrupulously anxious to please him, scrupulously anxious to conform.   And so she answered with a kind of serious playfulness now: ' That is my desire.'

'Very well, then, you will enter into my scheme of making our house something by itself, a point of light in the rather foggy intellectual atmosphere of Midlandshire. Without vanity, I think I may say that I am of rather different calibre to the ordinary hard-riding country squire, as you are of very different calibre to his wife.   And we must not permit ourselves to sink into the prevailing level, Mary.   Perhaps in saying that I overstep the limits of probability.   But even short of sinking to the level of our good neighbours, we might allow ourselves to deteriorate. *Entre les aveugles un borgne est roi.*   And we may be tempted to grow lazy and be content with a one-eyed royalty.   We must be on our guard against that.   We must be quick to note any signs of intellectual indolence. Too many women, after marriage, cease to cultivate their

accomplishments. You must not do so. You must continue
to read—we will read together. You must continue to paint.'

Mr. Aldham certainly had no cause to complain of lack
of due attention while making this speech. For Mary sat
watching him thoughtfully. And as she watched, her
sense of the obligation she had incurred towards him grew
very irksome to her. Paint !—the word, and she knew it,
knew it every day more clearly, irrefragably, held for her
the whole of a great rejected romance. In her present
humour, under present circumstances, she wished never to
touch a brush again. Yet there was her sense of obligation,
She had not had the courage to accept that romance.
She had made this man her way of escape from it. She
was in his debt. Moreover, but one line of conduct would
make life tolerable with him—the line of unconditional
obedience. So she said :—

'Very well. I understand. Reading will be delightful,
of course. And, if you wish it, I will go on with my
painting, such as it is.'

'Thanks. It is very pleasant to find you fall in so
completely with my views. I am all the more anxious we
should keep up to the mark in these matters, because in
politics we shall be compelled to lag behind. My uncle is
the staunchest of Tories. He and I agree to differ, on the
understanding that I also agree to be silent. During his
lifetime political society—such as we should both care for
— is impossible at Aldham Revel. But no embargo would

be laid on our entertaining literary people and artists. Therefore I should be glad for you to maintain a connection with any acquaintances of the kind whom you may have—with rising men like Mr. Colthurst, for instance.'

Involuntarily Miss Crookenden's eyes sought the place on the mantelshelf where dogToh had formerly been enthroned.

' Judging by the way his this year's pictures are spoken of, Mr. Colthurst is no longer a rising man. He is a very positively risen man,' she said. ' And we had better stick to the rising ones, Cyprian, I think, until we, too, have risen ; until Aldham Revel is a recognised second edition of Holland House, or Strawberry Hill. A little time will be needed to make it that, even though your calibre and mine is so very different to that of our country neighbours.'

Aldham raised his eyebrows slightly. Miss Crookenden's tone had a sudden flavour of sarcasm in it ; and sultans do not relish sarcasm from even the favourite light of the harem.

' My dear Mary ? ' he said slowly, interrogatively, restrainingly.

It was the first time her lover had ventured on rebuke. This rebuke was delivered courteously enough ; yet the girl winced and started under it, as a high-mettled horse will start under the gentlest application of whip or spur. She rose, and going to the table began arranging her presents again.

Aldham leaned back in his chair, in somewhat austere

silence. In his opinion Mary was distinctly in the wrong; it was therefore her place to make an advance in the direction of peace by speaking first. Some time, however, elapsed before the young lady saw fit to speak ; and then the subject she selected for conversation happened to be of a nature ill calculated to smooth ruffled plumes.

'I should be glad to arrive at a clear understanding about one matter, Cyprian,' she said, rather loftily, ' which so far has been neglected in all our plan-making. We have settled nothing about Sara Jacobini.'

Aldham rested his elbows on the arms of his chair, pressed the tips of his pointed fingers together and gazed at them with an air of withdrawnness and slight severity.

'I, too, should be glad to arrive at a definite understanding upon that point,' he observed.

'I take for granted you will not wish her to leave me.'

'That depends upon what you may mean by leaving,' he answered, slowly. ' You forget, perhaps, that you and I shall be my uncle's guests—guests on a peculiar footing which confers a good many privileges upon us, but still guests. To propose, as I proposed just now, we should ask agreeable people to stay in my uncle's house for short periods, is one thing. To offer to a man of his age and habits, as permanent inmate, a lady with whom he has not the slightest connection, is quite another. It strikes me that in doing so we should be making a rather excessive demand upon his hospitality.'

'Pray don't suppose that I have any wish to tax Sir Reginald's hospitality by forcing my relations upon him,' Mary said quickly.

Aldham ceased contemplating his finger-tips, raised his eyes to the girl's face. The sharp edge of his nature made itself very sensibly felt just then.

'We seem to be at cross purposes. That is unfortunate,' he said. ' Perhaps it would be as well if you explained your wishes a little more definitely. I really fail to apprehend them at present.'

' My wishes are very simple—that Sara should not lose her home; that I should not lose her.'

' The forming of new ties almost invariably necessitates the loosening of old ones,' Aldham remarked, a trifle—it must be owned—sententiously.

' Then, upon my word, I am not at all sure that forming new ties is not a mistake,' Miss Crookenden cried.

Aldham rose from his chair, keeping his cold blue eyes fixed on her.

' Do you in the least realise what your words imply ? ' he inquired.

But here, before Mary had time to reply, the conversation suffered interruption in the agreeable form of Violet Winterbotham. That brilliant little lady entirely refused to admit that her Easter campaign had ended in defeat. Not a bit of it. It had ended in a draw ; and she fully counted on resuming play on some future occasion.

Lancelot Crookenden had gone to shoot beasts and birds of sorts in Kashmir; but Miss Violet belonged to a section of society in which journeys are the rule rather than the exception. She had no doubt he would return safe and sound, all in good time; and the Kashmiree beauties gave her no anxiety. 'Mr. Crookenden wasn't *that* sort of man, you know,' she said to herself with meaning; and her meaning was a perfectly just one. In the interval she determined to keep his family well in hand; and in furtherance of this end displayed the warmest interest in the affairs of Miss Crookenden.

'Oh!—I know it's too bad to interrupt you like this, darling,' she exclaimed between effusive kisses on both cheeks—'because of course you and Mr. Aldham—how d'ye do, Mr. Aldham?—must have such loads and loads of delightful things to say to each other. And it must really be quite too odious for you to have people trotting in and out, specially in the morning. But I couldn't resist. Mr. Aldham, really I couldn't. I was simply expiring to see the new presents. She's got such lovely ones, hasn't she?'

Violet gave a sharp little cry; her manner became absolutely solemn.

'Why, Mary,' she said, 'what diamonds! Who did give them to you? What—what diamonds!'

'Cyprian brought them to-day from Sir Reginald. They were Lady Aldham's,' Mary answered, coldly.

Miss Winterbotham bent down over the velvet cases; then glanced up from under her pretty fringed eyelids with a look that had nothing in the least infantine in it.

' Ah ! they're family things—I see—heirlooms.'

She paused a moment, then broke forth again into innocent, overflowing enthusiasm.

' Well, I never saw anything so utterly lovely. Really, Mary, you are quite the luckiest girl in the world. Don't you think so yourself? I am sure I should. Aren't you frantically excited at having them ? I should be.'— Violet clasped her hands and beamed.—' I should want nothing more in life, Mr. Aldham, positively nothing,'if I possessed those diamonds.'

' Mary is not as easily pleased as you are. She regards her possessions from a very philosophic standpoint,' Aldham permitted himself to reply, as he shook hands with Miss Winterbotham.

' Ah ! this is quite too dreadful. I'm driving you away ? ' that young lady cried.

' No, I was going in any case.'

Violet moved aside, discreetly busying herself over the wedding presents.

' I wonder if they'd kiss if I wasn't here ? ' she thought. ' There, Mary's going after him. I hope she'll leave the door open; I should so like to see. Perhaps they'll kiss on the landing.'

But. Miss Crookenden made no offer of kissing her lover,

though she approached him in a spirit of most disarming
gentleness and apology.

'Cyprian, I am very sorry I have vexed you,' she said.
'Please forgive me. I spoke without thinking. Indeed, I
don't want to be troublesome or disagreeable. But life
seems such a hustle just now; and I get rather off my
balance sometimes. See, Cyprian, to show it's all right
between us and that you're not very vexed with me, will
you take me to the Academy this afternoon? I know I
have been tiresome about going there and fancied I never
had time. But I will make time to go there or anywhere
else you like to-day. And then we've a card for a
big party at Mr. Carr's to-night. I left the engagement
open, meaning to shuffle out of it. But perhaps you
would care for it? All sorts of people will be there—the
sort of people you were talking of having at Aldham. I
don't want to bother you; but I am quite ready to go, and
so will Sara be, if it would amuse you at all to meet them.'

Thus did Mary Crookenden strive to make it up with
Cyprian Aldham, and succeeded. For he accepted both
propositions.

'And to-night,' he said, 'you will wear the diamonds,
that is if you want to please me.'

'I do want to please you,' the girl answered, and her
grave voice shook a little from the earnestness of that
desire.

BOOK VI.—SATAN AS AN ANGEL OF LIGHT.

'Did I not tell you,' he said, 'that the jewel I had found was alive, and that it was a woman?'—*Papuan Legend.*

CHAPTER I.

ADOLPHUS CARR flew his kite with a long string to-night. For it was his happiness to entertain, not only persons, but a Personage. A Personage before whom you bent back or knee according to your sex; or despised and envied those who did so, not happening yourself to be among the number of the elect whom the said Personage graciously delighted to honour. Mr. Carr was very much in his element. He was a born courtier. His mind, civil to the point of indirectness, was quite at its ease in the extremely artificial atmosphere in which alone Royalty can exist. Not for a moment, however, must he be accused of being a toady. The courtier is as distinct from the toady, as the high comedy actor from the buffoon; or the cultivated Anglican divine—such as our friend Mr. Aldham, for instance—from the street preacher bawling rudimentary salvation on the top of a tub. Adolphus Carr was none the less suave, none the less confidentially polite, to the rank and file of persons present because of the Personage present likewise. But he exercised a refined diplomacy in respect of them. He displayed most commendable tact in marshalling them, in making them circle round the royal centre, in getting them to come and go, do and say, just all most calculated to please and amuse his royal guest.

And this was hard work. But Mr. Carr relished it. Relished, too, by anticipation—for why should we squeamishly seek to place lights under bushels when they may illuminate the hearths and homes of countless fellow countrymen if set in the great candlestick of the Daily Press ?—the very laudatory notices safe to appear (he had not forgotten to invite members of their respective staffs) in the Society Papers of the week.

It was not every day Adolphus Carr entertained Royalty, and he was prepared to spare no expense. He took pains, moreover, to acquaint himself with any little tastes on the part of Royalty which it might be possible to gratify ; and learning that his Hereditary Grand Duchess, in addition to her fondness for English letters and English art—which was easily enough gratified—possessed a fondness for white lilac, he loyally proceeded to turn his apartments into a garden and grove of those exquisite flowers. The night, for the time of year, was curiously hot. Three days of glorious weather appeared about to end in the thunderstorm, declared by our enemies invariably to give

a playful finish to a British summer. A weight seemed to
hang in the still air. And, as the hours passed and the
crush thickened, the rooms, notwithstanding their height
and long row of windows standing wide open on to the
balcony—it had been tented in with pink and maize-
coloured canvas, matted, supplied with seats, hung with
lamps—the rooms, I say, grew very much too warm for
comfort, while the faint, dreamy, all-pervading scent of
the lilacs became almost distressingly oppressive.

So it seemed to Mary Crookenden at least. She had
made due obeisance to Royalty, introduced Cyprian
Aldham to notabilities various and sundry, received con-
gratulations without number upon her approaching
marriage ; and now, having escaped from the crush, stood
fanning herself in one of the tall windows listening to a
lively stream of talk poured forth by Antony Hammond.

'At last, my dear Miss Crookenden !' he was saying
gaily. ' It seems a small eternity that I have been steering
my humble barque in the wake of your very august one
through this weltering sea of rank, talent, and fashion. I
thought I should never come up with you.'

Hammond, it need hardly be stated, was tremendously
on the alert as to the young lady's engagement. He was
most curious to know how the fair taker of scalps bore
herself under existing conditions. And it struck him now,
that her bearing offered rich harvest of suggestion to the
inquiring mind. Her dress was beyond all praise. That

white cut-velvet train—Hammond always knew what
women's gowns were made of—over its white silk and lace
petticoat, with its rather exaggerated scalloped silk *ruche*
at the bottom ; those sleeves reduced to the modest limits
—*pace* oh ! Puritans—of upstanding white velvet bows
on the shoulder ; those really magnificent diamonds ; the
lustrous though colourless complexion ; the delicate
brownish shading of the eye-lids—Hammond was ravished,
charmed. Afterwards, when people were talking a good
deal about Miss Crookenden and her doings, he greatly
relished describing her appearance that night.—'A sort of
glorious ghost,' he said. ' Impassive as Pygmalion's statue
before the silly fellow worried heaven into conferring the
doubtfully beneficial gift of life upon it. Miss Crookenden's
beauty was in the grand style that night. I assure you it
was absolutely prostrating.'

Immediately, however, Hammond exhibited no particular
signs of prostration. He chatted away brightly enough.

' As the vulgar little boys say, Carr has " got 'em all
on " to-night, hasn't he, Miss Crookenden ? This is his
social apotheosis. I feel quite weighed down by the
greatness of the occasion, don't you ? 'It is immense,
positively immense. Somebody ought to strike a medal in
commemoration of it. And you see the point of the joke
is, that no halt, no pause, no lapse is allowed in the
procession of incidents and attractions. The cry is still
" they come." Just now a *corvée* of Irish members—very

hairy—rushed in, the sitting being over or they possibly suspended for the night. A minute or two hence we shall be welcoming the actors, in their "mere capacity of man"—as the newspapers gracefully put it—and consequently very much the reverse of hairy, the performances at the theatre having concluded.'

Really the young lady's impassivity amounted to being slightly disconcerting, Hammond thought. She could hardly take the trouble to raise a smile.—'Is she craving, perhaps, for the society of the long-coated lover?' he asked himself. He whirled the string of his eye-glass round his finger, letting his easy light-hearted glance meanwhile wander over the crowd in search of the said lover. But Mr. Aldham was not visible. Hammond applied himself to conversation once more.

'It is hot—but hot,' he remarked. 'If Carr had altogether risen to the occasion, if he was quite the perfect host he aspires to be, he would have supplied each of us with a little lump of ice to wear on our heads, like the New York omnibus horses, to enable us to bear up under this kaleidoscope of excitements combined with this sweltering night. Ah! do just notice the angularity of Lady Theodosia Pringle's curtsey to the hereditary representative of crowns and sceptres, Miss Crookenden! The aroma of an earlier and more reverent age is about it. And now—really I must say Carr keeps the ball rolling with consummate ability—now, by way of contrast, we have the very last word of modernity in the shape of that anarchic, fire-brand of a creature—high priest of just' all non-strenuous souls like myself implore to be permitted to ignore and forget—James Colthurst.'

Hammond surveyed his companion again.

'Miss Crookenden, you are tired. I see it,' he said. 'You are bored. I know it. But do just oblige me by observing Colthurst behaving prettily to a Princess. There is a wealth of opposing sentiment in the situation which is delectable—very delectable indeed, if you permit your imagination to play freely around it. Believe me it is a unique little spectacle, one by no means to be missed.'

At last Hammond thought he had hit on a subject which interested Mary Crookenden. She turned her beautiful head, languidly and proudly, it is true, and gazed across the grove and garden of white lilac, past the groups of smart people, to the open space on the other side of the room where Royalty held its little court. But as she gazed her expression softened, her eyes dilated, kindled. Hammond talked on about Colthurst, the man's singular views, his extravagant tendencies, his doll-nursing idiot, his chain-harrowing boy; and Pygmalion's statue, meanwhile, showed increasing signs of animation. So he fancied anyhow. His curiosity began to be seriously aroused.

'That wretched idiot's face is as clever, in its way, as

the woman's in the "Road to Ruin,"' he went on. 'It holds a marvel of meaning. If his colouring and work-manship were not so superb, one would really be disposed to wonder whether Colthurst had not mistaken his vocation, whether he wasn't a great dramatist spoilt—'

But Hammond left his sentence unfinished. For here Miss Crookenden indulged in an odd and most unexpected bit of by-play. Drew up her hands with a quick shudder-ing motion, covered her eyes with her fan.

'Ah! ah!' she cried, softly suddenly; 'he has begun to stammer.'

Then she turned away, white cut-velvet train and all, and swept out of the window into the balcony, leaving Hammond literally with his mouth open, staring.

'Ye gods and little fishes, what is the interpretation of this?' he said to himself. He had never been more sur-prised in his life.

As we know, Hammond was not always very scrupulous where his curiosity was engaged, and just now his curiosity was stimulated to the highest pitch. It stood on tiptoe. Yet it appeared to him that common courtesy demanded that he should pause, give Miss Crookenden time to recover herself, that he should not do anything calculated to place her in a still more awkward predicament. He had the good taste, moreover, to extract all hint of inquiry and comment from his countenance before he followed her. When at last he did so, he tried to make as unconcerned, as light and airy, 'an entrance on the scene as might be.

'Yes, you are perfectly right to escape,' he said; 'those rooms are villainously, really fiendishly hot, and it is a shade cooler out here, I believe.'

The pink and maize-coloured canvas of the roofs and walls tinged the whole atmosphere of the long dimly-lighted place with a sort of amber glow. And through this, so it struck Hammond, Mary Crookenden's face showed singularly weary and care-worn, as she stood in her rich dress among the flowers with the cold brilliance of those superb jewels in her hair and upon her neck and bosom—a glorious, but really a quite uncomfortably ghostly young beauty. He had reckoned on finding her slightly defiant, as a woman usually is when she has betrayed something—Hammond used that vague term, for precisely what she had betrayed he was at a loss to determine. But Mary was not defiant. He could almost have believed she was frightened.

'O! it is terribly hot,' she said. 'The heat distracts me. It makes me quite ill. Have you any idea where Madame Jacobini and Cyprian Aldham are, Mr. Hammond? Will you help me to find them? I can't stay here any longer. He must take me home.'

'I won't help you to find Mr. Aldham, because—pardon a dogmatic tone, Miss Crookenden—I won't consent to your facing those basting rooms again. But I will find him myself and bring him here to you. Do you mind waiting?'

Mary hesitated.

'I don't know,' she said; 'I would rather go with you.'

But Hammond for once in his life was obdurate.

'My dear Miss Crookenden, be admonished! Don't venture into that furnace; you are evidently very tired. Sit down in the big chair yonder—you see?—right at the end. No one will molest you. They are mostly too busy staring at the Hereditary Grand Duchess; and Desborough is just beginning to recite some blood-curdling delight of a piece, which the lovers of emotion are trooping away to hear—just observe how they are all clearing out. You will be alone here and fairly cool. And it will take me precisely half the time to lay hands on Mr. Aldham if I go by myself. Find him I will, and that speedily, or perish in the attempt.'

Hammond smiled very pleasantly at the young girl. Her pathetic face taken in conjunction with her gorgeous attire made him feel deliciously sentimental. Little verses began to come into his head. Hammond quite hugged himself over the episode. But what did it portend? What, indeed what?

Mary made an effort to smile in return, but her lips were strangely stiff. The smile was not a happy one.

'Thanks so much. Please tell him I must go,' she said.

'Tell him not to be long, Cyprian is so deliberate. And I want to go home at once—at once.'

Chapter II.

Taken fairly, along with their context, the most astonishing affairs become comprehensible enough. The difficulty is to get hold of the context; and that is just why the conduct of even the most respectable of our fellow creatures presents to us such an endless tangle of contradictions, ineptitudes, inexplicabilities, and general wrong reason run riot.

Which observations find apposite illustration in the small affair, just recorded, which so taxed Antony Hammond's acuteness. To the one person able to supply the context—namely, Mary Crookenden—that affair was comprehensible to the point of humiliation. Precisely because she dreaded an episode of this description had she been anxious to 'shuffle out' of going to Mr. Carr's great party. Then her little quarrel with her lover had supervened. Wishing earnestly to make it up with him, to cancel their difference by presentation of some suitable peace-offering, she had defied the dread, risked the episode. And now, as she waited at the end of the balcony, the episode confronted her as an accomplished fact. She contemplated it in all its aspects and bearings; and, poor child,—poor for all her pride and fine clothing,—as she did so her heart grew heavy as lead. And unhappily she had plenty of leisure for contemplation, the wheels of Cyprian Aldham's chariot tarried most unaccountably. She could think undisturbed. For the chair to which Hammond had directed her, was shut in, hidden away behind a flowery promontory of white lilac bushes with an undergrowth of azaleas and gladiolas extending more than half the width of the balcony, and leaving only a narrow passage against the inside wall.

Mary Crookenden has retained a very lively remembrance of every detail of her vigil in that oppressively fragrant little spot. Of the six-sided red glass and brass lamp hanging in the centre, the chain of it vibrating slightly from the out draught. Of the rosy reflections cast by it upon the lilacs and azaleas. Of the slight clinging roughness—against her bare arm—of the pattern of the brocaded chair-cover, on which bunches of dim-hued carnations straggled across an ash-blue ground. Of the rich amber glow filling all the long perspective of the tented space. Of figures passing to and fro, or grouped about the windows of the brilliant rooms. Of the well-modulated murmur of conversation. Of the reciter's voice, now passionate, now appealing, rising in some declamatory passage, falling in some pathetic one; the tones of it singularly agitating—though the words recited were indistinguishable—amid the heat, the rich subdued brightness, the cloying sweetness of flowers. And then right before her—striking a very different note —an arched draped opening on to the darkness of the river and the night. Through this, as she sat there, she could just make out the line of the opposite shore. Lights reflected down upon the oily swirling water—current flowing, tide ebbing, away together past the roar and turmoil of the city towards the freshness and silence of the sea. Buildings, towers, great chimneys, black against a vague luridness behind them thrown upward, through the close thick air, from the network of teeming streets lying back between Lambeth and Vauxhall. Over all this another blackness of gathering cloud. Cloud big with storm, boiling up from south and east, though the wind was dead still. And in Mary Crookenden's mind meanwhile, sense of disquieting self-revelation, of moral confusion; sense, moreover, that struggle with that confusion only entangled her conscience and reason more and more hopelessly, as in the meshes of some cruel net. Not right and wrong, but right and right, not truth and falsehood, but truth and truth, appeared to her sadly in conflict just then. And it was of the very essence of the case that she could ask no advice, seek no counsel. Acting at once as advocate for each side and as judge, she must argue the question, give the verdict, bear—perhaps —the weight of long punishment, unaided, silently, by and for herself.

Yet the episode in itself remained comprehensible enough. She had honestly wished to avoid seeing Colt-hurst again, on this side her marriage at all events. Now she had seen him and her first sight of him had been alarmingly pleasant. It appeased her pride, it went to justify her past thought of him.—That word 'bounder' of Lancelot's had rankled in her mind.—For she saw that here, among all these people, Colthurst's personality re-mained distinct ; and that not by doubtful virtue of out-ward eccentricity, but by positive virtue of being an undeniably telling figure. Colthurst, indeed, had sloughed off much of his outward eccentricity in the last few months. The habit of rule, sufficiency of means, the comfortable knowledge of an assured success, had in-creased his social self-confidence and given him ease of manner. Looking, as he looked now standing talking to Adolphus Carr's Princess, Mary Crookenden felt he was not a man whom any woman need be ashamed of going into the world with. His appearance,· like his work, might provoke comment, but comment would hardly be of the patronizing, supercilious sort.

All this she perceived almost at a glance. Perceived it with an odd mixture of satisfaction and of uneasiness, knowing that she had infinitely better perceive nothing— that perceptions down these lines were dangerous, not to say wrong. Perceived it, moreover, with the glamour of those pictures of his, which she had looked at in company with Aldham at the Academy only a few hours ago, still strong upon her. For their virility, the consummate art, the large insight of them had affected her profoundly. And then, by an unkind little accident, as she watched him, listening all the while to Hammond's half-malicious, half-laudatory talk, it fell out that suddenly, unexpectedly, the attraction of Colthurst's weakness was added to the attraction of his strength. For looking about him, in that restless way of his, during a rather involved declaration of artistic faith on the part of the Royal lady, Colthurst's eyes had met hers. He became aware of her, aware she was watching him. The whole man had changed some-how. A certain excitement shook him. He began to hesitate in answering the declaration of faith, to stammer, and that badly. And perceiving this and how it came about, a desperation of pity, of anger that he should be at a disadvantage, of longing to help him, shelter him, stand between him and all possibility of ridicule, had arisen in Mary Crookenden, had made her cry out, and then, in shame and fear, had made her turn and fly. No wonder, I think, sitting alone, contemplating the episode in all its bearings the girl's heart grew heavy as lead.

Her first instinct had been to seek safety with Aldham, to get him to lead her out of temptation, to take her away. Now as she waited for him, while the air became more oppressive, the heat greater, the fragrance of the flowers more close and clinging—a presence rather than a scent—

that idea of the necessity of rescue amplified itself. Not only from this place, from the subtle influence of James Colthurst's near neighbourhood, must Aldham take her; but from all her old life, its associations, its aspirations, its surroundings, its fancies—and that as soon as possible. They were to be married—why wait? Why not be married at once? Only the completion of her trousseau stood in the way. And hadn't she plenty of clothes already? What did a gown more or less matter as compared with this horrible state of moral confusion? Mary was fairly terrified. To fix the great gulf of marriage—and to a high-minded young girl that gulf happily seems a very, very great one—between herself and the man who so strangely affected and attracted her—the man who told her he loved her and made her feel the truth of that telling as no man ever had before—told her also his love was hopeless, prayed passionately it might be kept so—the man in whose life was something obscure and hidden—Lancelot's hinted story, the haunting face of the woman of Slerracombe Deer Park—to place, once and for all, between herself and this man, solemn vows ratified by a sacred ceremony; to place between herself and him the mysterious change from maid to wife;—this seemed to Mary Crookenden her only chance of peace, of a quiet mind, of a conscience void of offence.

And, as the minutes passed and still Aldham did not come, this idea of the necessity for haste, for action immediate and final, deepened in her, possessed her, worked upon her till the nervous tension became almost intolerable.

No doubt Mary's distress of mind was aggravated by physical causes, by the highly electric state of the atmosphere. For, more than once while she waited, the whole southern heaven had opened for an instant —buildings, towers, great chimneys along the further shore standing out sharp-edged against a sheet of peach-bloom light. The river became mystically radiant, its bridges, the barges lying in mid-stream, the long pale line of the embankment as clear as day. For an instant only. Then the lamps which had grown pallid and ghostly re-asserted themselves. Night—there without all blank, black, stifling—here within, voluptuous with sound, colour, fragrance—closed down again.

A man's shadow thrown upon the lilacs and azaleas, doubled queerly by the crossing lights. Mary was past caring about appearances, past caring whether her words and aspect might seem peculiar to those ignorant of the context. She thought Aldham had come at last. She rose to her feet.

'Oh! Cyprian, Cyprian,' she cried, 'take me away, take me home now, directly, before the storm breaks.'

Rose, turned to the narrow passage between the banked-up flowers and the wall, to find herself face to face with James Colthurst.

'D-don't be afraid of the storm, Miss Crookenden,' he

said in the rapid whispering way of his. 'There is n-no hurry. I assure you it won't b-break just yet.'

And Mary sunk down in her chair again, a kind of despair upon her. Despair none the less honest and vital because she knew that at bottom she was glad, royally, triumphantly glad. Thus with jarring, discordant music, and in most questionable shape, does the great god Love batter his way into some women's hearts.

But the great god had only carried the outworks after all. For the girl's innate rectitude, loyalty, sense of the binding nature of a promise voluntarily given rallied and valiantly withstood the entrance of the enemy. If there is no treachery within the walls, why, the great god may have to retreat discomfited even yet. Mary could still resist, did instinctively proudly resist; but she could not take the offensive, make a sally, cut her way out. That was beyond her power of will. She waited silent, slowly fanning herself.

Colthurst had come within the flowery promontory. He moved across and looked away up the river watching the up-boiling cloud, for he did not care to look at Miss Crookenden just yet. He still cherished his dream of ideally chivalrous behaviour towards this woman. And he held it sentimental cant to assert that beauty when least adorned is most adorned. Not a bit of it. A woman's beauty gains by fine dressing, as a precious stone by fine setting. Colthurst knew that Miss Crookenden was re-

splendent to-night. He did not want to know more, to
know the details of that splendour, until the excitement of
finding himself here alone with her had somewhat worn
off. The emotional side of his nature was ready enough to
develop dangerous energy under existing circumstances—
and then the tones of her voice, calling out, just now,
as she supposed, to her lover, had cut him to the very
quick.

'The storm's a l-long way off yet,' he repeated, just for
the sake of saying something.

Mary made no answer. Colthurst paused for a brief
space. The heat, the fragrance, the silence in which he
became moment by moment more intimately sensible of
her, there, close by, the beauty of her person enhanced by
her appointments and surroundings—all this wrought on
him, produced in him a distracting restlessness. To carry
it off he began talking, caring little enough about the
subject so long as he did talk.

'You heard, I dare say, that I ended by taking the
Connop School ?'

'Yes, I heard you had taken it,' Mary said.

She fanned herself steadily. The regular mechanical
beat was helpful to the maintenance of self-possession.
And she, too, needed help towards that end just now.

'I hope the work goes on well ?'

'Oh! the work goes on well enough, Colthurst
answered with a certain impatience, still watching the up-

boiling cloud. 'I am weeding out the incapables by a p-process of inevitable natural selection which rather scares B-Barwell. He says I shall empty the school if I p-press the students so hard. B-but I don't agree. I shall only kill off the ones who have no stamina And I am p-perfectly willing to do that. I have no use for rickety creatures. Art has no use for them. I am d-delighted to help them to select themselves out of existence. I r-really am doing them a kindness in helping them to disappear.'

'Poor things!' Mary Crookenden exclaimed softly almost involuntarily.

Colthurst looked round at her. There was a curious fierceness in his expression.

' You think me b-brutal, Miss Crookenden,' he stammered.

'I don't think anything,' she answered, hurriedly, 'but that I am glad the work goes on well—that you should be satisfied.'

Colthurst gazed away up the river again. Once more the southern sky opened, and all the scene without showed clear. Whether it was only the change from the warm lamplight to that unearthly flickering pallor of the sheet-lightning Mary could not tell, but Colthurst's face seemed to her a revelation of how much sorrow a human countenance can hold. The sorrow was not showy, theatrical, obtrusive, but it was none the less penetrating for that.

'I am not satisfied,' he said. 'I longed for the school;

I thought I could do a lot with it. I got it. I am d-doing
a lot with it. I had my d-desire. I have leanness withal
in my soul. Why not ? The two things generally go together, I suppose.'

'Ah ! but,—' the girl put in eagerly—she could not help it
—the longing to comfort this strong, dominating aggressive
being overmastered every prudential consideration—it had
done so before.—'But there are your pictures. Surely
you find satisfaction in them ? I saw them to-day. No
other pictures in the place are within a hundred miles of
them. They are magnificent. They must satisfy you.'

'Of course I am p-pleased with them,' Colthurst said.
'Of course I am fond of them. Of course in a degree, I
glory in them. It would be a very paltry pretence of
humility to deny that. For no one can measure the worth
of his work like the artist himself—that is obvious, I
think. He only knows all that has been p-put into it.
Still more perhaps all that has been p-put out of it—rejected, refused. For the best work is always built up on
refusal somehow, on obedience to the "thou shalt not"
even more than to the "thou shalt." B-but then, just in
proportion as the work is good, complete in itself, an
actual creation, it becomes impersonal—is outside of you,
has an independent life. Your reason and your artistic
sense acquiesce in that. Your brain is content it should
be so ; your ambition is gratified.'

As usual, Colthurst's nervousness had off worn under

the relief of self-expression. He held himself upright, standing directly in front of Mary Crookenden, looking full at her.

'The m-man in you is satisfied, in short,' he said. 'B-but alas! there is a good deal besides the man in most of us artists. There is the child—the everlasting up-springing of youth, which is at once our curse and the secret of our power. And the child isn't satisfied. The child doesn't care two raps for laborious success, the creative gift, for acquiescent reason, or gratified ambition, Miss Crookenden. It cries out for toys, for p-playfellóws, for sunshine, and d-dear, silly little pleasures; a home to come back to at night when it's tired; l-loving arms to hold it; a lullaby of laughter and kisses.'

Colthurst's stammer grew somewhat unmanageable as he said the last few words. He looked down, wrenching oddly at his shirt collar.

'S-satisfied? Is anybody satisfied, I wonder?' he repeated. Then he raised his eyes to the girl's face. 'Are you satisfied, Miss Crookenden?' he asked, quite gently. 'If what one hears of your prospects is true—I hope it is —you have more cause for satisfaction than most of us. We hear you are going to make an ideal marriage—a marriage that has everything to recommend it, not a single d-drawback. Is it so?'

Mary fanned herself slowly, unceasingly. The heat seemed to her breathless.

'Yes,' she said.

'You are satisfied then ?'

Colthurst too found the heat breathless.

Ah ! self-confident and altogether too deliberate clerical lover, for pity's sake make haste ! If rescue is to be at all it must be speedy, for though the garrison holding the citadel of your mistress' heart shows a good front to the enemy, it is in sore straits.

Mary Crookenden stopped fanning herself. She carried her head haughtily.

'What right have you to ask me such a question ? You have no right,' she said, and once more the fan took up its steady rhythmical movement.

Colthurst looked down again.

'B-by a d-death-bed, Miss Crookenden, one doesn't stop to carefully consider rights. One acts upon impulse, regardless of conventionalities. Here by the death-bed of the love I have borne you I dare to ask strange questions—and if you are kind you will answer them. From the first I knew that love was doomed. It was not in the nature of things it could live. N-now it is in its agony. Very soon I shall be forced to lay it in its coffin and go on my way as best I can without the tormenting joy and solace of it. Don't misunderstand me,' he added. 'I am not making an appeal. I am merely stating facts. Facts of which I recognize the inevitable fitness as—well—as a fairly reasonable lost soul may be supposed to recognize the fitness of its own damnation. Only I think I should recognize that necessary fitness more completely—and, intellectually, anyhow, it would be a consolation to recognize it as fully as possible—if I had reason to believe you at least were happy. If I knew not only the woman-of-the-world in you is satisfied, but that the child is satisfied likewise; that it has found toys, a p-playfellow, a home— and that l-lullaby—and so is content.'

Colthurst spoke quite calmly. He stood near in the centre of the draped opening, his face and the upper part of his figure bathed in the dreamy amber-rose of the lamplight, showing in high relief against the gloom of cloud, and river, and night behind him. While across that gloom, now and again, the lightning leapt and flitted with, so it seemed to Mary Crookenden, a kind of evil quickness—at once a mockery and a menace, producing in her an indefinable terror. She hesitated, the apprehension of a great crisis upon her. Then in desperation of loyalty she lied; lied bravely, roundly, knowing that she lied, looking him in the face.

'Since you press the question home,' she said, 'yes, I am satisfied; I have found all I want.'

'Ah! that is well—d-damnation becomes almost palatable,' Colthurst said.

He leaned his elbows on the balustrade of the balcony, gazed down at the long row of carriages drawn up along the kerb each with its double dot of light, at the waiting men-servants chatting in groups on the pavement, at the swirl of the flowing current and ebbing tide. Colthurst had hardly realised until now how much it would cost him to screw down the lid of this love's coffin. The chill pride that had come back to Miss Crookenden's bearing in the last few minutes only charmed him the more. His relation to her all along, save during that interview in the drawing theatre of the Connop School, had been fantastical, shadowy, unsubstantial. Yet in closing it—and that truly honouring her he was called upon now to close it, Colthurst never doubted—it seemed to him that he parted with the best thing he had had in life.

A huffle of wind, hot with the festering reek of the crowded streets away across the river, fluttered the leaves of the plane trees along the embankment, swept up and about him, the stale odours borne on it for the moment overpowering the sweetness of the flowers. Then the air fell dead still again, while the thunder rolled and rattled away down in the south. The wind affected him oddly. To him it bore something beside the stagnant reek of the · streets. It bore a message from out of the stagnant profitless lives of Jenny Parris and little Dot. Colthurst was in the morbid humour in which it is possible to find absolute enjoyment in accentuating one's own suffering. A spirit of fantastic self-abnegation had possession of him. And so he asked himself—half from sheer hopelessness, half in obedience to the high ideal of conduct his love for

Mary Crookenden had generated in him—why should he
not right the wrong he had done Jenny in a measure at
all events ?   Why cling so determinedly to the fact of
legal freedom, since, with Mary Crookenden's marriage,
the one thing which had given legal freedom a certain
subjective value was irrevocably lost ?   Why not marry
Jenny Parris, and so take the stigma of shame off little
Dot ?   He had no love to give Jenny Parris.   She had
strangled all love in him.   She jarred him through and
through, every fibre of him, like the sound of an instru-
ment out of tune.   She could never be more than his wife
in name.   But his name he could give her.   He could go
to the nearest Registry Office with her, make—in her own
eyes—an honest woman of her; make his will too, settle
the not contemptible sum coming in for these pictures of
his on her and on his daughter, little Dot—and so pay a
part, at least, of the debt he owed her.   As the conception formed itself in Colthurst's mind, rapidly and with
curious completeness of detail, the vision it called up was
dreary, arid, dingy to the point of heart-break.   He did
not care.   To him, just now, the very merit of the conception lay in the vulgar commonplace misery of it.

The wind huffled again.   The thunder rattled out
somewhat nearer.   Colthurst raised himself, turned round,
a smile on his lips.   The contrast between what he saw
in imagination and saw in fact was sufficiently violent.
Mary Crookenden stood upright, looking away down the

length of the balcony—which was singularly provoking to
the senses in its cunningly blended colours, cunningly
disposed lights, flowers, furnishings—her beauty empha-
sized by her rich dress, her flashing diamonds, by the
stately pose of her figure and the carriage of her head.
Colthurst was filled with a madness of worship for her.
Not only of worship for her physical beauty, but for her
maidenhood, for the unstained fairness and purity of her.
The Registry Office and Jenny Parris—yes. But first a
word of kindness, a trifle of hope !

'Miss Crookenden,' he said, 'I have talked too much.
You want to get away from me. I d-don't want to
bother you ; but before you go just this.—I had some conversation with Mr. Aldham when I first came in to-night.
He tells me he cares for pictures. He was good enough
to ask me down to your future home—later, in the
autumn, you know, when you are settled there.'

The girl turned her head. And Colthurst remarked—
as Hammond had remarked already—that she looked
very fragile, ghostly almost. Her mouth was slightly
open, and an expression of startled alarm made her eyes
wide and wild. Twice she tried to interrupt, tried to stop
him. But Colthurst refused to be stopped.

'No—let me go on. It's a very small matter. Let me
go on,' he entreated. 'Don't suppose that I should be in
your way, or that I should demand more from you than
the most casual acquaintance among your guests. I

should be just an odd man in a big house-party, had down
to make up the number, to take any young lady in to
dinner who didn't happen to be better provided for, while
I paid for my keep in the smallest small-talk I could
raise. I know myself p-pretty thoroughly. I know what
is within and what is b-beyond my strength. This is
within it. I should be wholly unobjectionable.' Colthurst
smiled at her.—' Wholly unobjectionable,' he repeated.
' So my coming would make no difference to you, and to
me it would make just all the difference. It would be the
grating through which one catches a glimpse of the blue
sky in prison. It would—we were speaking of lost souls
just now, you know—well, it would be Judas Iscariot's
twelve hours' rest from hell in the cool and peace of the
polar night.'

His speech was low, broken, eager, to his hearer
cruelly moving.

Oh ! Cyprian Aldham, Cyprian Aldham, who shall
awake in you a sense of your danger ?   Rome is burning
while you, frigidly punctilious young gentleman, are
gracefully fiddling—fiddling to poor old Lady Theodosia
Pringle, whom your host has bidden you take in to
supper.   Will you risk losing your wife to save your fine
manners ?   In common modesty wait, at least, until she
be indeed your wife before you thus make display of your
self-respecting good breeding at her expense.   The flesh
has little enough power to tempt you, high-minded dainty-

natured person that you are.   But can we say as much for the world ?   Make haste, bestir yourself, hurry for once, putting your self-complacency in your pocket ; or I very much fear when at last you arrive, you will arrive altogether too late.

'D-don't blot out the scrap of blue sky,' Colthurst stammered.   ' Don't cut Judas off his twelve hours' respite from pain.   You have all you want.   You are satisfied, so to you it couldn't matter.   To me it would bring infinite good.   Let me come.'

But Mary Crookenden threw out her hands in passionate imploring rejection.

'Ah ! no.   God forbid.   Anything but that,' she exclaimed. Colthurst was keenly hurt.

'What have I done to you that you should hate me so ?' he asked fiercely.   'I don't deserve it.'

'I do not hate you.   It would be happier for me if I did,' Mary answered ; and then her voice rose into a cry.

For the storm had broken at last.   Broken in rough unseemly tumult.   Nature declaring her eternal supremacy even here, amid miles of brick and mortar, despite of buildings, pavings, bridgings, tunnellings, despite too of human millineries and masqueradings.   Broken, in blinding glare of lightning, and boisterous in-rushing wind that made the lamps sway and the tender greenhouse-grown lilacs writhe and shiver, and the draperies flap in wild confusion and tear at their fastenings. · While the thunder pealed out overhead—a deafening, metallic crackle and roar, that went booming away, volley upon volley, up the course of the river into the far distance. Followed by a downpour of rain—the great drops beating in, insolently careless of Adolphus Carr's elegant upholsteries; beating in till they splashed chill on the girl's bare neck and shoulders.

Mary had been wrought up to a pitch of emotion in which ordinary incidents take on most portentous colours. The flash and clap, coming at that moment, begot in her a panic of fear as of impending judgment; while the cold whip of the rain laid on her delicate flesh—so unaccustomed to the most distant hint of ill-usage—appeared an indignity, a cruelty, inducing in her a desolating sense of loneliness and friendlessness. So that it made the sobs rise in her throat, encircled by that brilliant weight of diamonds, even as wind and wet and callousness of nature to human distress make sobs rise in the throat of the ragged tramp huddled, shivering, under the hedge. All this was an affair of seconds. Then, though her eyes were closed—she had shut them to keep out the leaping glare of the lightning—she was aware of Colthurst close to her, standing between her and the in-beating rain, sheltering her, holding her hand quietly, with unaccentuated pressure, as he had held it once before. Aware that his presence, the personality and genius of the man, enfolded her, held her whole being spiritually as he held her hand actually in the steady clasp of his own.

One is told that in drowning, when the first instinctive passionate struggle for life is over, there comes a self-abandonment which is almost luxurious, a joy of yielding weakness the more exquisite because of the fearfulness of past conflict.   Mary experienced something of this just now.   The struggle of loyalty, the fight for independence were pretty well over.   Our proud, milk-white maiden began to drown peacefully, willingly, not indeed without a certain exultation.   The sobs sank away.   She opened her eyes, and looked with a sort of wonder at the lilac blossoms scattered on the ground, at the long length of the balcony, a queer effect of wreck and disorder upon it. The wind was falling again, the lightning was less vivid, and there were lengthening pauses between the thunder-claps.   Servants came hurrying out to tidy away the traces of disaster and close the tall windows of the rooms.

Colthurst quietly unclasped her hand.

' You m-must go inside out of all this,' he said.   ' The worst is over—and for me the b-best is over too.'

The note of hopelessness in these last few words aroused Mary Crookenden.   She ceased to drown peacefully.   The moral struggle was renewed.   But it was renewed on other lines.   She could not look her position fairly in the face as yet.   She was too close to it.   It was not possible to see it in the perspective which alone could make it intelligible.   But upon one point she was resolved her mind should be set at rest.   So she took her courage

in both hands, turned and asked Colthurst the question
plainly—baldly, if you will—which she had asked herself
a hundred times since the sunny afternoon in Slerracombe
Deer Park, when she had recognized them both—the man
and woman of the ' Road to Ruin.'

' Tell me,' she said, almost sternly—' what is the meaning of the despairing tone in which you speak about
yourself, about your life, about love ? Why is it ? Are
you married already ? '

Colthurst moved a step back, with a queer upward jerk of
his head as though he had been struck. He hesitated,
while Mary stood watching him, her eyes fixed on him ;
while the rain streamed down on the canvas roof; while
the servants moved to and fro, and the frightened carriage
horses backed and plunged in the street below. The cool
calculating side of Colthurst came to the fore. With
unsparing directness it put the case before him. To say
yes, and so save this woman whom he so dearly and
devoutly worshipped from all possibility of defilement, all
possibility of entanglement with these two sad, profitless
lives, bound up irrevocably with his own ? To say yes,
merely forestalling fact by a few hours, and give Jenny
Parris legal right to his name and to whatever of money
and position might go along with it before this day, just
beginning, had run out ? Or to say no—to repudiate
Jenny's moral claim on him once and for all ? To declare
himself free and take his chance ?—And what a chance !

What intoxicating delight that chance offered if he read Mary Crookenden's question aright. The rage of living was still strong in Colthurst for all his morbidness, for all his fanatic fancies. The thought of that chance made him set his teeth, while the blood throbbed through his veins like liquid fire.--But then again the risk of eventual misery to her. What had he said himself? The finest work is grounded in refusal; built upon 'thou shalt not' rather than 'thou shalt.' Was it so with the finest love? And then Colthurst saw that the most excellent way, the most splendid proof of his true love for Mary Crookenden lay in refusal—the most excellent way for him—good God! the tragedy, the bathos of it—led slap into the open door of the Registry Office side by side with the bastard and the harlot.

With a desperate courage he met the girl's serious, questioning gaze. Tried to tell her. Tried, in terms as little offensive as possible, to explain. But the words would not get themselves spoken. In his extremity his stammer once again became absolutely unmanageable.

At that moment two gentlemen came towards them. The foremost was Cyprian Aldham—Cyprian Aldham at last. Then the tormenting, debasing, insoluble riddle of sex obtruded itself, would take no denial, made its voice heard. And Colthurst fell. For the sight of Mary Crookenden's affianced husband coming thus to claim her, provoked in him the blind fury of jealousy towards a riva

common, alas ! to man and beast alike. His whole moral
attitude changed. The real rose up and murdered the
ideal, as in vigorous natures possessed of vigorous passions,
at times, it inevitably will and must. Not as some high-
exalted, spiritually-apprehended incarnation of inaccessible
maidenhood did Colthurst now behold Mary Crookenden,
but as sweet flesh and blood woman, to be wooed and won,
to be rejoiced over as bride and wife, to lie in his bosom,
and be at once—so strangely contradictory is man's desire
—his goddess and his property, his inspiration and in a
sense his slave. By a tremendous effort he mastered his
stammering tongue.

'Married ? N-no, no. Ten thousand times no,' he
said.

Chapter III.

The week following Mr. Carr's royal entertainment was
not one of precisely millennial peace and security to the
students of the Connop School. They went delicately,
like unhappy Agag, having a general sense of hewing in
pieces disagreeably imminent. Colthurst's moods, as we
are aware, had a habit of making themselves felt; and
his present mood was a peculiarly withdrawn and preoccupied one, out of which he seemed to rush at intervals,
as out of some cavern, armed with truly startling powers

of invective and mordant criticism. He was, it must be conceded, ill to live with during that week. But to no one worse to live with than to himself. For the end of his interview with Miss Crookenden had left him suspended, like Mohammed's coffin, between earth and heaven; and which of the two was designed to be his eventual resting-place he had as yet no means to determine. Aldham and Hammond had come, and Miss Crookenden had gone away with them. The whole business, so far as he was concerned, had been cut off clean, as with a knife.

How much her question had meant, for how much his answer might be taken to stand, the full significance of her declaration that it would perhaps be happier for her if she did hate him—on these cardinal points Colthurst was painfully in suspense. And he saw no practicable way of relieving his suspense. There were reasons in plenty, to his thinking, which rendered it obviously impossible for him to go and ask Miss Crookenden for explanations. And here Colthurst's underlying fatalism became of signal service to him once more. It enabled him to retain his mental equilibrium in respect of the issues raised by those cardinal points, it enabled him to 'stay put' in respect of the future. For, after all, what is to be, must be; you can no more hurry Destiny than you can delay her. One is always in plenty of time, dawdle as one may, for the Inevitable; that is a train one is perfectly safe to catch.

So Colthurst just sat down under his present suspense in grim patience, determined to await the event—not to act, as far as might be not even to think. But this Spartan-like resolution was by no means calculated to soothe an irritable temper; and so his near neighbourhood was certainly to be avoided rather than courted, during that week, by any anxious to keep whole the skin of their self-conceit.

Work is about the best anodyne for the dull ache of suspense, and Colthurst worked like a horse. Not content with the pictures he had in hand and the daily routine of the school, he took to attending the evening classes for male students usually carried on under the mild auspices of Mr. Barwell. And he dropped in to one of the said classes for an hour one night on his way to a 'small and early' dance at the Frank Lorimers'. Colthurst was not very much in the humour, as can easily be credited, to go and make sport for the social philistines ; moreover his enthusiasm for his prospective host and hostess was always of the slightest. Mrs. Frank's pretty little person and shew, self-sphered, impenetratable little nature vexed him. He knew she regarded him very much as a bull in a china-shop ; and, by natural fatality, in her presence, something of a bull in a china-shop he only too frequently became. Still, the Lorimers were friends of Miss Crookenden ; and Colthurst's Spartanism did not carry him so far as to prevent his being willing enough to embrace any opportunity of hearing news of that young lady which might present itself. So he went into the school duly arrayed for the festivity ahead; though all the same the prospect of the said festivity was so little alluring that his tongue and temper were highly distinguished for the reverse of suavity during that evening class. The students heard him close the door of the theatre with relief. Even Mr. Barwell had been somewhat mauled; and now the good man followed him, along the flagged passage and up the stone stairs, very much in the spirit in which a faithful dog, that has endured an unjust beating, trots sadly reflective at his master's heels.

'It's p-positively disgusting,' Colthurst was saying, as he reached the top of the flight; 'they haven't an ounce of imagination b-between them, I believe. B-but I could forgive that. P-people aren't responsible for being born fools. What I can't forgive is their want of application.'

As he crossed the hall the porter put a note into his hand.

'It was sent on from your rooms, sir,' he said. 'They said the person who brought it begged you might have it at once.'

Colthurst took the note mechanically, and went on to the office.

'In that, I must say, the female students, notwithstanding their affectations, are a lot the pleasantest to deal with of the two. Even the stupid ones have the merit of being more or less in earnest.'

He moved across to the gas-jet over the office table and held the note up to the light. The address was in pencil. It was in Jenny Parris's not very scholarly handwriting. It was something new for Jenny to send him notes. The hard line cut itself deep across Colthurst's forehead. What the devil did she want ?

' I suppose we may hope to see one of our most earnest young ladies back again before very long, at this rate,' Mr. Barwell observed mildly.

He clasped his lean hands under his coat-tails, and rested his back against the wall. The under-master was rather done up, rather hurt; yet still, in his amiable way, he made an effort to give the talk a less growling tone.

' She threw us over for matrimony ; but now, if report speaks truly, she has thrown over matrimony in its turn. So we may hope she will return to her first love.'

Colthurst stripped the envelope off the note, and turned up the gas, which hissed and spluttered for a moment. Jenny's writing was almost illegible.

Meantime Mr. Barwell continued his small remarks.

' I shall be glad if she does return, for she was distinctly one of our best workers ; and a young lady of her standing helps to keep up the tone among our students. And then too '—he added, ' I'm an old fellow, so there's no harm I think in my saying it—it cheers one and does

one good to see so charming a sight as she is sometimes.'

The under-master shifted his long back into an easier
position against the wall, smiled and then sighed involuntarily. Even his gentle unexacting nature rebelled
somewhat against the on-coming of Old Age, its depriva-
tions, humiliations, disabilities. For him life had had no
splendid, no tremendous hours. It had just been a steady
piece of collar work along an extremely ordinary road.
His share in the romance of the worship of art had been
confined to sweeping down the steps of the temple, and
teaching novices their a, b, c. The making of music
within, the celebrating of the mass, had been for others.
And now Old Age laid its hand on him, and whispered
that even sweeping the temple steps, even teaching lazy
scholars the rudiments, would soon be better done by
younger men. Colthurst had confirmed that whisper
to-night, in the drawing theatre; had hinted, in a moment
of irritation, he was getting past his work. The good man
was sore.

' Yes, selfishly, I hope she'll come back here,' he said;
' for I should derive my own private modicum of pleasure
from the return of Miss Crookenden.'

To the first part of this little discourse Colthurst had
not been attending; but at the last few words he was
round with a sort of flash, while the ill-written, crumpled
sheet of note-paper fluttered down to the floor.

'M-Miss Crookenden coming back here? What d-do you know about her coming back?' he stammered.

'Oh! I have no authority for asserting that she will return here,' Mr. Barwell answered, a good deal flurried by this unexpected display of fireworks right in the middle of his sentimental reflections. 'Only, as I learn she has broken off her engagement, it struck me as not improbable—'

Colthurst could not restrain himself. 'W-where did you learn that?' he demanded.

'From yesterday's paper—the *Morning Post*,' Mr. Barwell said, not without a touch of dignity. He resented—really he could not help resenting—this very abrupt and hectoring form of address. 'My sisters happened to see the paper at a friend's house, and having heard me speak of Miss Crookenden they informed me of the announcement.'

'I beg your pardon for cross-questioning you'—Colthurst made a strong effort to subdue his excitement— 'b-but I had not heard the news. I know Mr. Aldham, and so it has a special interest for me. What exactly was the announcement?'

'That the marriage arranged between—I forget the gentleman's name—Oldham—Aldham, yes, Aldham you said—and Miss Crookenden would not take place. That was the wording as reported to me.'

Mr. Barwell left the kindly support of the office wall,

went towards the door with his shuffling walk. Colthurst's small apology had mollified him, gone far to restore his momentarily wavering allegiance; but the hand of Old Age pressed upon him, there was no question about that. He grew so fatigued of night now—quite longed for the repose of the semi-detached villa and affectionate ministrations of the gentle parrot-nosed sisters at Hampstead.

'Well, good night, Mr. Colthurst,' he said. 'I hope you will enjoy an agreeable evening. I must go down to those idle young gentlemen of ours. I suppose we shall welcome you at the accustomed hour in the morning.'

'Of c-course—yes—good-night,' Colthurst answered absently.

He sat down at the office table, rested his elbows on it, leaned his head in his hands. For a good twenty minutes he remained peacefully in that attitude. Through the prosaic medium of a daily paper Mary Crookenden had informed all whom it might concern that her proposed marriage was broken off. She had probably done this to put a stop both to congratulatory letters and speeches, and to the arrival of wedding presents. The reason mattered little enough to Colthurst, it was the fact he hailed, just the bare, simple fact. It quieted him as opium quiets. For the time it filled him with a rapturous calm, in which all his faculties rested in a state of enchanted inactivity. The fact was enough in and by itself as yet.

But the western mind cannot long remain in this condition of trance-like beatitude, thanks to the vexatious impatience of the western body. Downstairs the model was leaving; and a confused noise of talk and movement in the theatre marked the breaking up of the evening class. Colthurst rose to his feet, stretched himself, took a long breath. Outside the soft brooding twilight lingered even yet. He thought he would wait until the students had departed,—Mrs. Frank Lorimer's 'small and early' was out of the question now, an insult to taste and intelligence—and then he would go out and walk. Walk, it didn't much matter where. Walk, till the brief obscurity of the summer night melted into the fair summer dawn, and to-morrow awoke and climbed up the rosy eastern sky. 'Beloved to-morrow' as it seemed to Colthurst just then—though precisely what he counted on to-morrow bringing him, he was, at present, too content to care to ask.

Crossing the office to fetch his hat and overcoat, his foot slipped slightly on a piece of paper. Colthurst stooped and picked it up; and with a quick, sickening revulsion of feeling saw and remembered Jenny Parris' note. He hesitated a minute, then went back under a gas-jet to read it.

'I would not ask you for myself,' it ran, 'after what's past, but Dot's ill and goes on mourning for you all the while; she's your own child, you know, Jim, and the doctor says it's a question if she lasts over the night like she is now.'

What ! are you turned jade and hussy all of a sudden,
'beloved to-morrow,' lifting your veil thus before the time
and showing a glimpse of something singularly unlovely
lying in your lap? Colthurst put on his hat and overcoat, set
out on his walk.   Not to some opium-eater's fine-fanciful
love paradise, but down St. Martin's Lane, through West-
minster, on by dreary shabby-genteél street after street
south-westward to Delamere Crescent.

CHAPTER IV.

JENNY PARRIS was at her best in illness, unselfish, patient,
self-forgetful.

'Drink it down like a good little maid,' she was saying
as Colthurst came in, and her voice was sweet with a
sober, motherly tenderness.

But the lodging-house sitting-room looked even less
attractive than usual,—the table in the middle of it
cluttered up with medicine bottles, a finger bowl of rapidly
melting ice, a half emptied tin of jelly, a basin of toilet
vinegar and water, the cleanly scent of which struggled
but unsuccessfully against the tainted air of the room.
Jenny's gown had been flung down, anyhow, upon the
arm-chair by the fire-place ; while she, arrayed in a black
alpaca petticoat and pink flannel jacket (very much past

its first youth) sat, a fine unself-consciousness and absorption in her whole attitude, leaning over the horse-hair sofa
on which Dot lay.   The neck of the little girl's night-gown
gaped open, showing her flat childish bosom ; her back
was propped up with bed-pillows ; and a Mexican blanket,
once white with a magenta and black border and centre
piece to it, now of somewhat indiscriminate hue, was
wrapped about her feet and legs.   Steve Kingdon had
brought that blanket home to his sweetheart long ago,
from Manzanillo on the Pacific Coast.   And Colthurst
loathed it with a consummate loathing ; for it had been
the most substantial, at last the only, covering of his own
sick bed during that waking night-mare of a time in the
garret of the *Hotel Garni* in Paris, now just four years
back.

'Drink it down like a good little maid,' Jenny repeated.

And Mrs. Prust, standing at the foot of the couch, all
kindly, blinking, fussy solicitude, echoed the refrain.

'Yes, take it all down, there's a pretty dear.   Captain
Prust 'ull be as pleased as never was to hear Dot's took
her physic like a sensible, good child.'

But poor Dot was not more amenable in sickness than
in health.   She tossed her head to and fro with the restlessness of semi-delirium.   Her eyes were closed, her
usually pale cheeks all of a flame, and her lips almost black.

'I don't want no nasty old medicine,' she fretted, 'I
want to go away.   I want to go where it's pretty.   Every-

thing's so poky here. I want Mr. Snell to come and take me to see the ladies dance. Where's Jim? Why don't you fetch him, Mammy? I tell you I wants Jim.'

Mrs. Prust pursed up her mouth and shook her head, until the chenille blossoms decorating her cap vibrated wildly. Colthurst had entered the room very quietly, her attention was claimed by the child and her back was towards the door. So was Jenny's for that matter. But she had no need to be told when Colthurst came into the house. She knew his step as he passed along the pavement, knew his ring at the bell; felt his coming bodily, right through her, with a bitter, yet delicious spasm and stab.

'Well, you can have what you want, then, that way,' she said, quietly; 'Jim's here.'

'What, Mr. Colthurst—never,' the landlady cried, wheeling round. But she restrained further comments, congratulatory or the reverse, for in truth Colthurst's present costume impressed her considerably. And, as she subsequently informed her master-mariner downstairs, though she 'didn't hold with Mr. Colthurst's goings on, and never had, she was bound to say, and if it was her last word on earth she'd say it, that he looked every inch a gentleman to-night and no mistake.'

Meanwhile Colthurst examined the sick child.

'What's the matter with her?' he asked.

'Typhoid fever,' Jenny said, over her shoulder without

moving. 'She's been awful bad this last week. Clean out of her head by times, telling all manner of fool-ishness.'

Here Mrs. Prust found a dab absolutely irresistible.

'And her poor mother all alone with her, night and day, till she's properly wore out.'

Colthurst glanced at the speaker not quite pleasantly.

'I think we can dispense with your p-presence now, thank you, Mrs. Prust,' he said. 'I p-propose remaining here to-night and helping to nurse Dot.'

Then he put aside his hat and overcoat, drew one of the shiny horse-hair chairs up beside the sofa, silently took the wineglass of medicine from Jenny. He slipped his left hand, out-stretched, under the nape of the child's neck and thin shoulders raising her slightly; while, at his touch, she made a queer little croodling sound of comfort. Jenny Parris had known the calming, sustaining quality of that touch before now. She never expected to know it again. She had not seen Colthurst since the evening following her luckless visit to the Connop School, and she feared that that day's work had made a breach between them past closing. And so hearing the child's croodling cry, understanding just what it meant, poor Jenny began to feel a hungry jealousy all crossbarring her mother love. She watched, as a jealous person invariably watches eagerly that which most greatly inflames them, a dry light in her grey eyes.

And through Colthurst too, that odd, half animal intimation of solace sent a rather painful thrill.   Taken in
connection with the sight of the old Mexican blanket, with
the sight of Jenny's handsome haggard face and untidy
attire, taken in connection with the news of Mary
Crookenden's broken engagement, it struck home, shook
his nerve.   A minute or more elapsed before he quite
cared to trust himself to speak.

' L-look here, Dot,' he said at length, ' I have come and
I'll stay and help you to get well.   B-but you must do as
I tell you.   You must drink this.'

' I don't want any more nasty old medicine,' and the
child began to toss her head from side to side again.   ' I
wants you to kiss me, Jim.'

A flush came over Colthurst's dark skin.

' Very well, I'll kiss you, b-but only when you have
d-drunk your medicine,' he said.

She fretted feebly ; and, in Jenny Parris, witnessing her
helpless suffering, jealousy died down and mother love
once again rose paramount.

' Poor little mortal, humour her, Jim.   For God's sake
don't teaze her any more.   I can't stand it.'

' If I am to manage her at all, I must manage her in my
own way,' Colthurst answered.   He held the glass to the
child's mouth again.   ' D-drink it, Dot, and then I'll kiss
you.'

' Oh ! you'm cruel hard,' Jenny cried.

She got up hastily, went to the table, turning her back on him ; heard the little girl's sobbing protest, the man's unmoved insistence, then a gulping struggle to swallow on the part of Dot. Jenny pressed her clenched hands against her chest. It was just all she could do not to drag the glass away, not to make a scene with him. Yet when the gulping was over, and she, looking round, saw Colthurst kissing the child, her thin arms clinging about his neck, jealousy once more invaded Jenny Parris. She would have given her soul for a kiss just then, had such unholy bargain been feasible.

' Oh! nurse me, Jim !' Dot moaned out, as he raised his head. 'I likes to be against you. Your clothes smell so lovely.—Mammy's clothes always smells of nothing but the cupboard. And this nasty old sofa's so knobby. I can't never go to sleep. And I'm so tired—so dreadful tired.'

When the wailing voice ceased Jenny stood for a moment motionless. Then she threw back her head with something of her old, generous, impulsive daring, and came across to the sofa again.

' Take and nurse her, Jim,' she said, ' there's a good fellow. Sleep's the thing to cure her if she's to be cured. And you can put her to sleep if you've a mind to ; like you can do anything else when you've the mind.'

She snatched up the Mexican blanket and arranged it over his right arm and his knees.—' That's to save your lovely clothes,' she said, not without a dash of mockery.   She stooped down, lifted the little girl, tenderly, skilfully, and placed her in Colthurst's arms.   Stooped lower and wrapped the loose end of the blanket about her feet.

' Put her to sleep, Jim,' she said, huskily.   'Cure her. She's a wicked little thing ; but she's yours as well as mine, and she's all of you I've got left—now.'

And Jenny went and flung herself down in the arm-chair by the fire-place.   She kept her eyes fixed on Colthurst's, profile, on his bent head, on the sweep of his broad shoulders, as he leaned a little forward cradling the child ; followed his every movement with insatiable attention, motionless, save now and then when a fit of coughing shook her, for Jenny's cough had been troublesome of late, and her handkerchiefs, too often, had come to be stained with blood.

Colthurst, meanwhile, steeled himself against her scrutiny, doing his best to concentrate all his thought upon the little girl, whose body, dry and burning from fever, felt like a hot plate lying across his knees.   In his deft way he stripped up her night-gown sleeve, and began passing his finger tips softly round the palm of her hand, up as far as the hollow of her arm and down again to her wrist.   But at first the mesmeric charm refused to work.   To make it work, the operator needs a disengaged mind; and Colthurst's mind was rather horribly preoccupied.   For, after his absence of some weeks, the mean, littered room, all that it stood for, all that it implied, its tainted atmosphere, struck him with a freshness of repulsion, of remorse, of rage against himself, that he had gone and made this thing, this ugly cage as of unclean birds, wherein, from time to time, it was ordained his soul must come and sit. Even his natural pity for the sick child was doubled with a kind of spiritual disgust; for he saw in her the poisonous fruit of his own sin—an evil deed taking on bodily form and confronting the doer of it as a material fact ; saw in her the incarnation of his own lust and Jenny's ruin.

And so, not unnaturally, at first he failed to soothe Dot. Every few minutes she opened her eyes and broke into rambling, disjointed talk.

'I wish you'd come and live along of us, Jim,' she said, presently. 'It's all so dull now you don't never come. —What a lovely clean shirt you've got.'

And Dot wriggled her restless head about till her hot cheek rested against the cool, smooth surface of Colthurst's shirt front.

' I love's you better 'n any one,' she went on. 'Much better 'n Mammy. Mammy's always so mopey.'

The leather cover of the arm-chair creaked as Jenny shifted her position.

' B-be quiet, Dot,' Colthurst stammered.

' Oh, let her talk. You needn't be considerate of me. It's a bit late for that. And I'm pretty well used to that

sort of talk—hear it most days,' Jenny said, recklessly;
and then the dragging cough took her.

To Colthurst all this was inexpressibly painful. He
could not sit still under it. He got up and began walking
backwards and forwards the length of the two rooms, for
the double doors were open into the bed-chamber, carrying
the child in his arms. He hoped movement might serve
to still Dot; but on went the relentless little voice.

'I wish you'd come and live along of us,' she repeated.
'I wish you was my father.'

'Hush, hush,' said Colthurst.

'But I do. I loves you better'n anybody. And the
children in the street throws it up against me I ain't got
no father.'

'Do they? The little devils!' Colthurst murmured under
his breath. He felt rather beside himself.

Just then his walk brought him opposite to Jenny. She
lay back in the arm-chair, exhausted by her fit of coughing.
Her breathing was irregular and laboured. She pushed
the dark masses of her hair up from her forehead and
wiped her face round with a very shaky hand. The light
from the gas over the table fell on her. She looked
ghastly; Colthurst seeing her softened somewhat.

'I'm afraid you're ill again,' he said.

'That's an old tale,' she answered, her lips parting in a
half-defiant smile.

'B-but have you seen a doctor? Has he p-prescribed

for you ?   Have you taken what he ordered ? ' Colthurst
asked.

'Doctor's stuff's not much use for my complaint.'—
Jenny's eyes met his, her smile sweetened, quivered, died.
—'The white witch over to Nettlecombe used to give the
maids a draught to keep true love,' she said, slowly ; 'and
I'm thinking that's the stuff as 'ud do me most good, Jim.'
—She wiped her face round again, and her voice grew as
shaky as her hand.   'But up here in London they don't
know how to set about making medicine like that.   They're
a deal too wide-awake to believe in such a pack of old
foolishness, and so— '

Her speech was interrupted by another fit of coughing.
Colthurst walked on into the dusk of the unlighted bedroom, and sat down on the edge of the disordered, unmade
bed.

'Oh my God ! what must I do, what must I do ?' he said.

Again he thought, and seriously, of the Registry Office ;
but that, so it seemed to him, did not meet the require-
ments of the case.   It would cripple him, mutilate, and
stultify the possibilities of his life, and yet fail to satisfy
Jenny.   For Jenny wanted not his name but his love.
And that she should have his love was impossible, out of
all nature and reason, they standing to each other in the
relation in which they now stood.   Colthurst, in his
present extremity, could have resigned the hope of ever
drawing nearer to Mary Crookenden ; but to resign it to

no purpose—that seemed too much. Then Dot asserted the fact of her sad little existence once more.

'I want to go away where it's pretty,' she repeated, fretfully. 'It's all so ugly here, and the children's bad to me.—There's children as wears lovely short frocks and sashes tied low down, and I'd like to play with—but they drives me away,'—Dot's fretting rose into crying—' 'cause they says their mothers says Mammy's a kept-woman, and so they mustn't 'sociate along of me; and their frocks is lovely—and they've got a doll's pr'am—and I wants to play with 'em awful bad. Why's Mammy like—'

At first Colthurst had not been conscious of the drift of her talk, but he had gathered enough of it, and more than enough now. He laid his hand on the child's mouth, and, with a dislocating sensation of mingling pathos, shame, abhorrence, felt her parched lips kiss and re-kiss the palm of it. Verily this was a vile thing which he had made, a horrible place wherein his soul must come and sit! For a moment his courage gave out. The skein seemed too tangled for any disentangling. The old longing took him for rest and peace and escape at any price. Then by one of those immense acts of will, in which the energy that should rightly go to cover some weeks of living is expended in a few seconds, he pulled himself together, got up; went back into the sitting-room again, placed himself on the sofa, raised his hand from the child's burning, kissing mouth, bent down over her, looked her in the eyes.

'You shall go away, where it is p-pretty, go away for a long while,' he said. 'But to be able to go you must get well, and to get well you must sleep. Do you hear? you are to sleep, Dot—to sleep—listen, to sleep.'

And once more he began stroking her wrist, his fingers moving slowly up to the hollow of her arm and down again; with the result that as the heavy minutes passed she grew quieter, her eyelids drooped, closed, while her breathing became more regular.

But Jenny, unluckily, had misinterpreted Colthurst's whole course of action, thought him callous, thought he had gone away into the bedroom to avoid her, thought he had returned now to show his indifference to her suffering. And so, seeing him bend down and speak in that low whispering way of his to Dot, jealousy, rivalry of her own child again tore her. Yet, so strangely does mother-love overrule even the headiest passion, she waited until she believed Dot to be safely asleep, and then hardly spoke above her breath.

'You didn't make yourself so smart just out of compliment to us, Jim, I reckon,' she said. 'You go out most nights now to some grand doings or other, I expect. Fay! I wouldn't mind having a chance to go to some of 'em too. I'm like Dot, I want to go away where it's pretty.'—Jenny rubbed back her rough hair, and her voice took that taunting ring again.—'Suppose you tell about it all, Jim,

while we sit here so nice and quiet. It 'ud help to pass
the time a bit.   Where were you off to to-night?'

'To Mrs. Frank Lorimer's dance,' he answered,
succinctly.

'I'm sorry we spoilt your pleasure by sending for you
down to our poor place,' Jenny returned.   'Seems quite a
pity, doesn't it?   And who were you going to dance with?'

Colthurst had been studying the magenta and black
border of the Mexican blanket while Jenny was speaking.
Her tone, the rasping incongruity of his whole position,
maddened him.   He turned wicked.

'With no one,' he said.   'I d-don't dance in these
days, not even to a b-barrel organ on the doorstep, like
my sweetly-brought-up little d-daughter here.'

'Ah, that's a bad one,' Jenny cried out, sharply.   And
Colthurst was forced to own to himself it was an extremely
bad one.   But that was precisely why he dreaded and
recoiled from this unhappy woman so.   She had a fatal
capacity of bringing out the very worst in him, of driving
him to do and say all that was most repugnant to the
finer taste and nobler nature in him.   And it was just
this capacity of Jenny's which in his opinion constituted
her unpardonable offence.   She had a demoralising effect
upon him.   It is comparatively easy, under certain conditions, to forgive our neighbour his own trespasses; but it
is well nigh impossible to forgive him the trespasses he
makes us ourselves commit.

But here Dot created a diversion, and this time a fortunate one. During the above conversation, low-toned
though it was, she had become increasingly restless. Now
her limbs twitched and started, and her eyelids opened
partially, showing the whites of her eyes.

' Oh ! I'm so thirsty, Mammy,' she moaned. ' I'm all
like I was on fire inside of me. And the penny-ice man
with the red and blue waggon's up along the street. Give
me a penny, Mammy.—Oh! he's going, he's going, why
ever ain't you quick ? '

At the first moaning cry Jenny was on her feet. She
came across, knelt down in front of Colthurst, put a spoon-
ful of Jelly to the child's mouth.

' Poor little soul,' she said, softly, while with character-
istic absence of ceremony she planted the jelly tin on
Colthurst's knee. ' Catch hold of it, Jim. Perhaps she'll
take in a bit more if I try her; and it's the first mortal
thing that's crossed her lips but a drop of water and the
medicine you gave her these twelve hours.'

So there he sat, our man of genius, our devout lover of
a pure maiden—and surely there was a good deal of
heroism, a good deal of nobility, in the position ? holding
the tin of jelly, holding Dot; Jenny kneeling before him,
while the fronts of her old pink flannel jacket swept against
him at every movement, her rough hair almost brushed his
face, while patiently, tenderly, forgetting self, forgetting—·
harder thing by far to a woman—the close proximity of

the man whom she adored—in obedience to the divinely excellent instinct of motherhood, she fed the sick child.

In spite of himself, Colthurst was touched.—' Look here, Jenny,' he said, quietly, 'I have no wish to quarrel with you and behave b-brutally to you. Your case is pretty hard, b-but, before God, mine isn't much better. The principal difference is that your wretchedness has no lie in it, is all of a piece. Whereas mine has a showy outside to it—is a sepulchre, of which the world as a rule only sees the staring white-wash ; while I see, with an endless nausea, the dead men's bones and all the uncleanness lying rotting within.'

' I don't want no more, Mammy,' and Dot turned away her head fretfully.

Jenny stood up, took the tin from Colthurst, waited a moment looking down at him out of tragic grey eyes.

' Let's cry quits, for to-night at least, for the child's sake,' he went on. ' We brought her into the world to please ourselves, and were a pair of consummate fools for our pains ; but that's neither here nor there. Now don't let us risk adding murder to the old sin, by letting her slip out of it again while we are busy gratifying our very natural inclination for slanging each other. I can't argue with you and soothe her to sleep both at once. B-be reasonable. Leave me alone. D-don't badger me. You must see that lengthening the long score we have run up against each other won't really do either of us the faintest good.'—

His tone became less bitter.—' Go and lie down—get some rest. It is clear enough you need it ; and leave me in peace to do my best for the child.'

It was past five, broad day, when at last Colthurst let himself out into the street ; the long, confused, distressful night was over, with all its warring emotions, its cruel strain and fret. The little girl lay sleeping on the bed in the back room. And Jenny slept too, in the arm-chair by the fire-place : her left arm raised, her hand under the back of her head, her full lips pouting, her forehead drawn into a frown beneath the unruly masses of her dark hair, while her bosom rose and fell in quick catching breaths. Large-limbed, statuesque even now, though wasted by disgrace, sorrow, and that dragging cough, she looked like some worn passion-torn Maenad, with—for the fashions of the ages change queerly—rusty black alpaca petticoat in place of fawn skin, and, clasped in her right hand for the thyrsus, the plated tea-spoon with which she had fed little Dot.

CHAPTER V.

Dot did not die. Such superfluous members of society rarely die somehow, but she had more than one bad relapse. Her illness was stubborn, it cost Colthurst time, thought, and money ; for he continued to do his duty by the child in a spirit of dogged patience. More than one night

he sat up with her, and went away in the early summer
mornings dazed and spent, to take up his day's work at the
Connop School.   He led a curiously dual life during this
illness of Dot's, and he found it very distracting.   Sometimes when Jenny, over-wrought by anxiety and watching,
losing sight of his present kindness in the memory of past
wrongs done her, let loose her tongue upon him, Colthurst,
to borrow his own rather violent phrase, had reason to
congratulate himself on being in pandemonium well up to
the neck.   He had heard that Miss Crookenden had gone
out of town.   He knew no more than that ; and it seemed
to him, under existing circumstances, there would be a certain grossness in trying to find out more.   All that must
stand over for the present, probably stand over for ever.
Residence in pandemonium does not tend to generate a
hopeful frame of mind.

Meanwhile, invitations continued to pour in upon Colthurst, for he remained very much the fashion during that
season.   His flavour was a pungent one, and therefore
welcome to Society's rather jaded palate.   He was famous
and consequently was *fêted.*   Pretty women petted him—
or, to be accurate, did their best to pet him, for Colthurst
was not an animal altogether easy to pet—and when he·
treated them to some rather blasting sentiment, pro-
nounced him to be "really most deliciously quaint."   All
this caused him much bitter amusement, and his existence
seemed to him most thoroughly of the sepulchre sort.

And so time drew on until the summer term ended, and the Connop School closed for the vacation; but Colthurst remained in London, waiting until Dot should be sufficiently convalescent to be sent off to the seaside with her mother. It was not until the first week in August that the child was strong enough to be moved. Colthurst went to Delamere Crescent on the morning of her departure; saw her and Mrs. Prust and Jenny and a very miscellaneous assortment of luggage—a sea-chest, rickety band boxes, bulging brown paper parcels—bestowed within and upon a four-wheel cab *en route* for Waterloo.

He watched the cab drive off—Dot putting her pale little face out of window and kissing her hand effusively to him —with a dreary sense of accomplishment, of dull relief. This business was over for the present, any how, and he was thankful. But he had a feeling of utter depression upon him. It was over, but only to begin again later in some other form. He was not rid of it, only rid of a phase of it. And as Colthurst wandered away by the mean, shabby-genteel streets down to the Embankment, in a purposeless fashion very uncommon to him, he asked himself savagely whether the next phase might not be worse even than the last.

The day was not calculated to dispel depression. It was overcast, colourless, while everything seemed coated by all-pervading dust. Even the river looked dusty, running low and sluggish, fouled here and there by great floats of

iridescent scum.   In few places can you be more completely
alone than in London in August.   To Colthurst the solitude
was not unwelcome.   He had had only too constant companionship of a kind lately.   The unwholesome moral and,
indeed, physical atmosphere he had breathed, the conflict-
ing emotions induced in him by Dot, the strain of constant intercourse with Jenny—of behaving decently to her
yet keeping her at arm's length—had told on him, for the
moment had drained his vitality.   He felt utterly empty,
as though he had no volition, no power of recovery or re-
bound left.   He sat down on a bench facing the river, took
off his hat, and stared aimlessly at the slow drifting
scum.

' I am regularly played out,' he said.   ' Jenny and
circumstances combined will be too much for me, after all.
And the thing which rules this great lie of a world, God,
devil, blind force or Fate—whichever it is—is unjust, unjust.   It picks out a victim here and there at random, to
make an example of, while it lets a score of others, whose
crimes are just as black, get off scot free.   And it has paid
me the very left-handed compliment of picking me out,
placing me among the examples.   I have done no worse
than numbers who marry and settle, as the phrase runs,
and flourish like green bay trees and produce whole groves
of legitimate small bay trees ; while scandal never raises a
finger against them in the way of revelation of a doubtful
past.'

Colthurst turned his head, looked along the bench. At the further end of it a man lay sleeping, his face pillowed on his folded arms.

'Yes, the thing is unjust,' he repeated, 'unjust. You and your next-door neighbour are guilty of precisely the same lapse. To him, in the long run, it makes not a fraction of difference, while you are hounded to death.'

He gazed sullenly at the man lying along the bench, a disreputable figure dressed in what had once been good clothes—that sorriest of garments a seedy frock coat— the leg of one trouser, moreover, hitched up, showing that he wore no socks, had nothing on his feet save a pair of cracked and dusty old patent-leather boots. Colthurst, observing him, was affected by a despairing sense of brotherhood.

'There is another victim,' he said. 'Another poor wretch made an example of—hung up like a crow by one wing in a cornfield to warn other crows of filling their crops with forbidden pleasures.'

He looked back at the floating scum.

'By heaven, I should be glad to know how low it is the intention of the Thing which made me that I am to fall? Am I ordained to sink and sink, till I too come to lie on a bench in broad day on my stomach, in the few clothes I have saved from the pawn shop, and drown the shame of a great failure in sottish sleep?'

Colthurst got up.

'There's always one remedy in reserve,' he said. 'Nothing can deprive one of that, but want of pluck; and so far whatever I have lacked I haven't lacked pluck, I think.'

He went on, the same drained dead-alive feeling upon him. It was an ill-starred morning, whatever was grotesque and unsightly appeared to have come forth to display itself. All the cripples seemed to be out and about, all the slatternly women and girls, the tails of whose tattered skirts lick up the refuse of the pavement; all the underfed, scrofulous children; all the broken-winded, spavined horses. And everywhere, on everything, thick and choking lay the penetrating London dust. He turned off the Embankment just short of Battersea Bridge into the wider and more fashionable streets. But the dust was there too. The houses were blank and silent, blinds and shutters closed, plants withering neglected in window-boxes; the road-ways vacant, arid, desolate. Lamentable sights claimed Colthurst's attention here also; at last, among others, the very lamentable though very common sight of a cat playing with a wounded mouse.

When he first remarked the creature, she was perfectly quiet, save for the tip of her tail softly lashing the grey flags; while the mouse deluded by her quietness, crawled from between her outstretched paws to reach imaginary shelter in the gutter under the edge of the kerb stone. For a second or two the cat let the fugitive be; rolled over and over in rather diabolical gaiety, with those

queer feline chucklings of enjoyment that it is quite the
reverse of comfortable to hear.   Then she found her feet,
leapt lightly after the mouse which had just gained the
gutter.   And Colthurst, though by no means the most
sentimentally soft-hearted of men, turned sick, as he saw
the poor little beast sit up on end, squeaking thinly sharp
as a slate pencil squeaks when you draw it upright across a
slate, and strike out right and left at the cat's great, grinning, whiskered face with its tiny fragile-fingered paws.

Colthurst felt mad against the cat, forgetting that, as
cats go, she was really quite within her rights, for in
her dealings with the mouse he read a rather ghastly
parable.   So he struck at her too, tried to drive her off;
but she proved too quick for him, nipped up the shrieking
mouse in her white teeth, and bounded away across the
road and down between the area railings of a house opposite.   Colthurst followed her, a singular necessity upon
him to witness the end of the tragedy, and as he did so
the aspect of the house in question arrested his attention.
It was painted pale blue, its window-boxes were fresh,
still charming with flowers, the dust seemed to have found
no lodging-place upon it or them.   With a sensation at
once happy and sinister, Colthurst perceived it was Mary
Crookenden's house—the house he had once visited, and
from which he had been ejected rather ingloriously, thanks
to Madame Jacobini's liberal use of the snuffers.

For some minutes he paused in the middle of the silent

roadway. This morning he had reached the bottom of
his great discontent; now the reaction came, as in such
a nature it was bound to come. For the rage of living
had suffered but temporary abatement in Colthurst. He
shook himself queerly as though actually to shake off and
rid himself of the lethargy that held him.

'After all,' he said, 'a mouse, here and there, must
make good its escape. Perhaps, after all, Fate has not
loaded the dice. I will try one throw more, for the
chance of salvation through the love of a pure woman.
Injustice may go far, but it can hardly dare strike her to
compass my punishment. That would be too flagrant.'

And then, thinking of Mary Crookenden, Colthurst's
flesh cried out for her; and not his flesh only—for Satan
tempting him had at least the grace to tempt him through
the nobler as well as the baser side of his nature—all that
which was spiritual in him, ambitious of what is lovely
and of good report, cried out for her too. He went
across the dusty road, a tremendous revulsion of feeling
upon him. Rang, enquired for her, learnt she had rented
a cottage down in Surrey for the summer.

Colthurst took the first hansom he could find and rattled
down to Waterloo. He would go and see Mary Crookenden; ask her to be his saviour, ask her to be his wife.
He told himself he had been scrupulous to the point of
mania. He must have her; for she only could save him,
save in the truest and deepest sense, his life.

Out in the country there was sunshine, a rich profound green of woods, and gold of corn-lands. Out in the country there were no grotesque and sinister sights, no clinging, choking soil of dust. As the train whirled away through the sunny landscape, Colthurst was filled by a glorious renewal of hope. And yet he remembered, though he fought against the remembrance, how, while he stood on Miss Crookenden's doorstep, he had heard the cat growling to herself down in the area as she crunched up the mouse.

CHAPTER VI.

Do you know what it is to love and be loved ? Do you know—not by hearsay merely, but by experience--this absorption of the life of one human being in another, the one man in the one woman, the one woman in the one man ? For the time they, each to each, alike the centre and the sum, the very end and purpose of creation; the rest vague, phantasmal,—they, each to each, the only abiding reality. For the time they, each through the other, possessors and interpreters of all things; this immense universe a setting merely, the sights and sounds, the glory and wonder of it, but ministers to their delight in one another. For them stars rise and set, and the wheat waves under the summer wind. For them the sea grows white westward, at evening, meeting the sky in long embrace. For them all fair pictures are painted; all songs sung; and even common things become instinct with a strange sacramental grace. For them the oracles are no longer dumb, the mysteries lie open, they walk with the gods.

This is the crown and triumph of the riddle of sex; wherein, for the time, the long torment, shame and anguish of it is forgotten, so that man's curse becomes, for the time, his most .exquisite blessing—a blessing in which body and spirit equally participate. Whether, rightly considered, we here touch divinest revelation or most malign illusion, who shall say? But, for the time, that is a detail; for the illusion, if illusion it be, is complete.

Colthurst lay—not on his stomach on a dusty London bench—but on his back in the springy heather, his hands clasped under his head, looking up at the mackerel sky. Somewhere far away in the depth of the wood, a wood-pigeon cooed, cooed—most reposeful of natural sounds. And now and again a draught of air hushed through the fir-trees, and stirred the delicate foliage of the birches fringing the edge of the plantation. Mary Crookenden sat very still, her feet crossed, her hands in her lap. A long slanting ray of sunlight, from between the ruddy trunks of the firs crowning the ridge behind her, gilded the shadowed brightness of her hair. In the hollow, some few yards below, was a shallow moorland pond. And her eyes, fixed on the smooth surface of the clear brown water, were lustrous, serious, with a great content.

For this was one of those good hours when love grows perfect to the casting out of fear. She had no dread of the man lying there on the heath beside her. His strength no longer oppressed her as it formerly had done. It seemed to buoy her up, she rejoiced in it. Just now the troubles that her choice involved, the opposition of relations, the possible severance of old friendships, her Aunt Caroline's inevitable anger, Lancelot's inevitable distress, all the talk that the announcement of this new engagement following so hard on the heels of that other broken one necessarily provoked—these were forgotten. Only the mellow serenity of the September evening, the magical charm that haunted the still woods, the dry warmth of the light moorland air, the sense of the man's great love encircling, upholding her, remained. And that love now was not fettering, constraining, impeding; for she had yielded herself up to it with a fulness which had converted it from bondage to freedom. Mary Crookenden had never been more self-secure, more serenely proud in the days of her loneliness than now when she had given her heart irrevocably into another's keeping.

A couple of big red dragon-flies flashed hither and thither over the little brown pond, on the smooth surface of which the blue sky, dappled with cloud, was reflected. A swarm of gnats danced upward, in a tall, shifting sunny pillar. A sighing passed through the upper branches of the Scotch-firs. The wood-pigeon ceased cooing. Mary turned sideways, rested her right hand on the heath just beyond Colthurst's shoulder, leaned right across between him and the sky, looked down at him with triumphant fearlessness.

'Are you happy?' she asked.

'Divinely,' Colthurst answered.

'Are you satisfied?'

'Almost,' he said.

The girl bent her beautiful head and kissed him, smiling with a certain gentle gravity.

'Now are you satisfied?'

'Ah! my beloved, my beloved,' Colthurst murmured. 'Ah! my beloved,—your face and behind it the eternity of that blue sky.—No, there are only two more things to ask for—the day and night that make you my wife, and then—then if it might be—last and best gift of God, d-death, "delicate death."'

Mary drew back.

'Then you're not happy after all,' she said. 'For the last thing one asks being happy, is to die.'

'I d-don't know about that,' Colthurst said.

'But you must be happy,' the girl insisted. 'What more can I do to make you so?'

' N-nothing, except never change, never love me less.'

There was a silence before Mary spoke. Her eyes were on the quiet little brown pond, and again from the heart of the wood came the soft cooing note of the pigeon.

' I can never love you less, because to me you and love are one and the same.' The girl's face flushed. ' I can't think of it apart from you, or you apart from it,' she said.

Colthurst raised himself on his elbow; and, while he looked up at her, for one of the first and last times in his life his eyes filled with tears.

' And yet,' he said presently, stammering suddenly— ' yet I am not the m-man you ought to have loved, whom you ought to marry. Sometimes, even now, I have a hideous d-dread that you have stepped off the right lines of your nature, that you will find out that you have suffered a d-delusion, and then—then '—Colthurst laid his hand on her knee—' my p-precious one, are you sure you've counted the cost ? '

' There is no cost, now,' the girl said.

' Not here and to-day, perhaps, but later ? You may come to hear things about me. P-people may tell you ugly stories.'

' I shall not believe them.'

' But I have lived hard,' Colthurst went on. ' It's true. I have got scars, n-nasty scars. As time goes on you may happen to see them, they'll shock you, disgust you perhaps.'

Mary shook her head, still looking at the bright shifting pillar of dancing gnats.

'B-but they are not honourable scars, many of them. I got them fighting in no particularly glorious battles.'

Colthurst stretched his hand further, laid it on her hands as they rested on her lap.

'You m-must understand now—it is right you should understand, though it is dreadful to me to tell you. B-before I knew you, I was vicious, I was p-profligate. I never d-drank, but only because drink never happened to tempt me. And I never scamped my work either, b-because till I knew you it was the only thing I really loved. But the sins that did tempt me, I committed. And sometimes the remembrance of them rise up hot in me, and defiles all the present. And then I feel guilty of sacrilege in b-being near you, in touching you, in letting you kiss me as—bless you for doing it—you kissed me just now.'

Colthurst's hand closed down on hers, gripping them until he almost pained her.

'You have r-raised me,' he said. ' You have brought my whole life up to a higher level. B-but still the Ethiopian can't change his skin or the leopard its spots. I shall do and say that at times, however careful I am, which must be displeasing to you, which must offend your taste.'

His grip on her hands tightened. A strong desire was

upon him, it had grown and grown during the past month of close intercourse—to make a clean breast of it and tell her all; for the more he delighted in her the more he recoiled from dealing dishonestly with her. And yet how was it possible, plainly and positively, to tell her this thing?

'I have been penniless, and that leaves a scar, leaves an abiding distrust of the good faith of fortune, even when she comes to one, as she has come to me lately, all b-broad smiles, and her lap full of gifts. I have starved.'

'Ah!' cried the girl, with a little movement towards him.

Colthurst smiled at her. Her pity was very lovely. But he went on.

'Yes, it is not agreeable to starve. That leaves a scar too. It makes you envious, makes you cruel, makes you feel murderously towards your well-fed fellow-creatures.' He paused a moment.—'I have herded with outcasts. Have been dependent—God forgive me, for I didn't know where the cursed money came from then—upon the earnings of a common——'

But Mary, almost violently, drew her hands away.

'You hurt me,' she said.

She rose to her feet, moved slowly down over the carpet of purple heather, and stood, a tall, slim, stately young figure, on the shore of the little pond. Then Colthurst's purpose melted into thin air. For all his life, all the worth and purpose of it was bound up with this woman; he clung to her as the devotee clings to his god. There was an almost superstitious element in his love; even momentary alienation such as this gave him a sense of despair. Surely, he reasoned, things having gone thus far, his first duty now lay in preserving her peace of mind? Surely the burden of self-accusation, the burden of disclosure, was lifted off him if she thus refused to hear? He waited a minute watching her, undecided. The gnats danced on and the pigeon cooed; and the light became more ruddily golden as the sun sunk behind the firs, making their branches glow like living flame. Then he went down and stood near her beside the little pond. And out of the clear brown water her face looked up at him pale, questioning, sad. Colthurst was cut to the heart.

' I'm a b-brute,' he said, in that quick, urgent, whispering way of his, ' a selfish brute to have troubled your sweet soul with the story of my bad days. Thanks to you, those b-bad days are over, for—for ever. We will b-blot them out of remembrance; from now they shall be as though they were not, never had been. Forget all I was mad enough to say, put it away from you. And forgive me, Mary, as you love me—if, indeed, you do love me—forgive me. Trust me, my darling, I will never pain you like this again.'

Colthurst stretched out his arms to the fair image in the water; and as he did so, the face looking up at him

lost its sadness, began to smile with a certain grave
tenderness.

'My b-beloved,' he stammered, greatly moved, 'my
beloved.'

Just then a ripple passed across the surface of the pond,
breaking and distorting the reflection ; but that was of
slight moment to Colthurst, for he held the woman herself
in his arms. Her head was on his shoulder, her heart
beat against his heart.

' I do love you,' she said, ' I can't help myself. I don't
want to help myself. Whatever you may have done,
whatever has happened to you—I can't help myself—it
makes no difference. Only please don't tell me, that can
do no good, and—I'm cowardly—I'd rather not know.'

And Colthurst put his hand on her white throat as her
head lay back on his shoulder and swore a great oath she
should never know. To save her from that foul knowledge
he would lie, and if needs be do worse than lie. For his
passion made him wholly unscrupulous just then, reckless,
blind to all obligation, but the one of sheltering her. And
he hated Jenny Parris, hated the thought of her, hated the
fact of her existence, with a consuming hatred. For her,
crossing Mary Crookenden's happiness, he had no mercy.
She must be obliterated, and, along with remembrance of
his old bad days, utterly blotted out.

Half way home, on the edge of the great common—
where the moorland ends and civilisation and its restraints

in the shape of banks, and lanes, and high-roads begin—
Colthurst stopped.   Critical common-sense as represented
by Madame Jacobini was waiting, as he only too fully
realized along with other restraints of civilisation, just
ahead.   He looked at the young girl earnestly, almost
fiercely through the dimness of the mellow September
dusk.

‘You are satisfied?’ he asked in his turn.   ‘You have
no regrets?’

Mary shook her head.   ‘Now, none,’ she said.

‘Now, yes.   But to-morrow, next day?’ Colthurst
demanded.

Mary glanced round.   They were alone, but for the long
dark stretches of the moorland, the churring of the night-
jar, the round-headed oak trees in the hedge.   And, so
thoroughly had the great god Love taught our proud,
milk-white maiden his strange lesson, that she took Colthurst's face in both hands, drew it down, kissed him once
again on the lips.

‘For those who love as we do, as long as they are
together it is always now,’ she said.   ‘So that to-morrow
and the day after matter not one little bit.   Only don't
ask to die, my dearest, just as you are making me understand all that it may be to live.’

BOOK VII.—THE WAGES ARE PAID.

'Sail forth—steer for the deep waters only,
Reckless O soul, exploring, I with thee and thou with me;
For we are bound where mariner has not yet dared to go,
And we risk the ship, ourselves and all.'—WALT WHITMAN.

CHAPTER I.

THE philosophy of the point of view is a great and illumi-
nating philosophy; but it tends somewhat to the promotion
of pessimism, showing, as it does, the permanent and surprisingly great gulf fixed between one human mind and
another. For instance, while James Colthurst and Mary
were thus interpreting creation by means of their love for
one another, that love struck some persons as an anything
but desirable piece of business.

Mrs. Crookenden settled her large shoulders back in her
wicker chair, planted on the gravel just outside the Slerracombe greenhouse, and addressed her brother-in-law in
tones of profound displeasure.

'My dear Kent,' she said, 'it is useless to attempt to
explain away the disagreeables of this new departure on
poor Mary's part. This is the climax of a long course of—
you must excuse my saying so plainly—most extraordinary

and inconsiderate conduct ; and shows a most lamentable disregard of other people's feelings.'

Mrs. Crookenden folded her hands, with their array of handsome rings, over her crochet, and drew her chin in.

' It is most unbecoming, most unbecoming.'

The Rector was in low spirits. His tongue had lost the keenness of its edge. And he found nothing better to reply than—' Well, if she is making a mistake, poor child, she will be chief sufferer by it, in any case.'

Mrs. Crookenden, gratified by this indirect concession, picked up her crochet again, and continued calmly :—

' Breaking off her engagement to Mr. Aldham was bad enough, caused discomfort and annoyance enough, I am sure. Poor dear Miss Aldham can't get over it. It is quite sad to see her. And most awkward for me. She sent for me the other day, and, I'm sure, I did not know what to say. You see the engagement had been made so very public, he had gone about with Mary so much. Everyone knew about it. I consider her behaviour perfectly unpardonable.'

'You would have preferred her marrying Aldham and being more or less miserable ?' the Rector inquired.

' If she was miserable it would have been entirely her own fault. She would have had an excellent position. Mr. Aldham is a most thorough gentleman. I really don't know what right Mary has to ask more than that. Most girls in her circumstances would be only too thankful to make such a good marriage. Mary has a most undue

opinion of her own importance, I am afraid,'—Mrs. Crookenden folded her hands again,—' but then she has been
spoilt, dreadfully spoilt.'

The Rector drew little patterns, crosses and squares and
intersecting circles, upon the gray shingly gravel with the
point of his walking-stick.

' Yes, perhaps I have been to blame,' he said, quietly.
' There's no fool like an old fool, you know, Caroline. Very
likely I have done Mary more than one ill-service, fancied
I was going the way to make her young life pleasant when
I was really only pampering myself.'—His mouth twitched
into a rather harsh smile.—' More than half the love for
our friends and neighbours on which we plume ourselves
so much, proves to be nothing better than self-love when
we run it to earth. Egotism is a slippery customer, difficult
to catch, it doubles and turns like a hare.'

Mrs. Crookenden congratulated herself, she really found
her brother-in-law surprisingly reasonable and amenable
this afternoon. And this praiseworthy frame of mind of
his raised her hopes ; for Mrs. Crookenden once having
conceived a purpose did not easily relinquish it. Placid-
natured people are usually obstinate. All through these
years she had clung to her original scheme for the disposal
of the Rector's hand and heart. Lady Dorothy Hellard
still unmated, continued to trot after her very tough old
mother, the dowager Lady Combmartin, up and down this
troublesome world. Mrs. Crookenden cherished a belief

that only her brother-in-law's exaggerated devotion to his niece, had prevented poor Lady Dorothy's tired middle-aged feet trotting into the open door of Brattleworthy Rectory and there finding rest long ago ; and in proportion as Mary got out of favour, it appeared to her that such highly desirable trotting might even yet be effected. She therefore amiably proceeded to blacken the young lady to the best of her ability.

'My dear Kent, pray don't run away with the idea that I think any blame attaches to you,' she said, graciously. 'Everybody has combined to spoil poor Mary, and put her rather out of her place. And then I never can admit that Madame Jacobini is quite refined and so on, don't you know. I always feared she might put very odd ideas on certain subjects into a girl's head. And, I think, it has proved so. But all that doesn't lessen my feeling about Mary's behaviour to you.'

'Behaviour to me ?' the Rector inquired, quickly.

'Yes, in making a marriage you disapprove of, after all your extraordinary generosity to her.'

'You take my disapproval for granted ; but I have expressed none, as far as I am aware.'

Mrs. Crookenden moved in her chair with slight impatience.

'Of course you disapprove, everyone must disapprove who has Mary's welfare at all at heart,' she said, in her large official manner. 'She had the chance of making an extremely good marriage, and in a fit of caprice throws it all aside for the sake of some extraordinary artist, drawing-master sort of person, whom—well, really whom one knows nothing in the world about.'

The Rector began to cheer up. His sister-in-law became amusing. To her, he knew, as to such a very large section of our fellow country men and women, the arts are and always will be, I suppose—it belongs to the Anglo-Saxon race—pretty much a matter either of dancing dogs or the finishing governess.

'It is a very odd marriage for a girl who has had her advantages, a very poor marriage.'

'Mr. Colthurst is prepared to make better settlements than I anticipated,' the Rector said.

Then Mrs. Crookenden saw her opportunity, she spread all her canvas. In she sailed.

'I am delighted to hear it. Because then I really do hope and trust, my dear Kent, that you will begin to think a little more of yourself. I consider that your life has been completely sacrificed to Mary's extravagance, and to her pleasure. Now I do trust you will not make her that enormous allowance any longer. If she marries this man, let her live in a way suited to her position. She has some money of her own ; that and what he makes —I suppose that sort of person really makes a good deal —ought to be quite enough for her. It must be enough for her. You ought to be set free.'

Mrs. Crookenden glanced at her brother-in-law. She never felt quite safe with him, somehow, when it came to close quarters. And his aspect just now was not encouraging; his under jaw protruded, and his eyes followed the geometrical figures he described on the gravel with the point of his stick. Mrs. Crookenden disliked extremely to see the gravel made untidy, but she dominated her sense of annoyance.

'Let her begin at a suitable level,' she went on.

'Who is to determine what level is suitable?' the Rector inquired.

'Oh! that is easily determined by the amount of her income—her own real income. And, meanwhile, my dear Kent, you must begin to live at the level of your real income.'

'Buy more tobacco than I can smoke, more books than I can read, more horses than I can ride,' he said. 'I increase my establishment, collect a number of greedy servants about me, and give them nothing to do?—No thank you, Caroline. I am better as I am.'

'There are other ways of spending money,' Mrs. Crookenden said. 'My dear Kent, the subject is not an easy one to approach with you. But you know how often I have tried to speak to you about it.'

The Rector leaned back in his chair.

'What subject?' he inquired.

'That of marriage.'

Mrs. Crookenden paused. The Rector doubled himself together and fell to drawing those, to his companion, very irritating patterns again.

'Yes,' he said, 'I daresay it is difficult to approach. We all shelter ourselves, you know, Caroline, as best we can ; are most stand-offish where perhaps we feel most strongly. Frankly the subject of marriage is an unwelcome one to me. I'd rather leave it alone. But let me just state my opinion to you plainly. A marriage of reason has always appeared to me a wretched travesty of—well, of a very beautiful thing ; a travesty so wretched, that no person respecting his own intelligence could be guilty of lending himself to it. For the only justification of the very peculiar relationship we take so calmly for granted under this name of marriage, is love. And for a man of my age to fall in love is little short of indecent.'

' Really, Kent,' Mrs. Crookenden exclaimed. She was very much shocked.

' Therefore,' he went on, ' though I regret Mary's choice in some ways, I have acquiesced both in her breaking with Aldham, and in her present engagement. She is making a considerable venture, I know ; probably there are diffi-culties for her ahead. My object is to make those difficulties as little irksome as possible in the only way I can, namely, by securing her a comfortable and suffi-cient income quite independent of her '—the word stuck in his throat—' of her husband. She will, therefore, receive precisely the same allowance she always has received.'

'She ought at least to know that it is an allowance, and not her own,' Mrs. Crookenden said. 'She ought to be told the truth.'

The Rector completed a very elaborate curly-cue on the grey gravel.

'I shall not tell her, and, pardon my saying so, I shall be seriously annoyed if anyone else does so.'—His tone changed, he turned to his companion very courteously.— 'You have always been a kind friend to me, Caroline, and in this little matter you will respect my wishes, I feel sure.'

He leaned back, stuck his chin out, and his thumbs in the armholes of his waistcoat.

'We all have our trifle of romance,' he said. 'And my trifle happens to be bound up with Polly. It will remain bound up with her to the end of the chapter.—Now let us talk about something else. What news have you of Lance?'

Mrs. Crookenden had picked up her crochet. The enamelled lockets rattled rather aggressively as the tortoise-shell needle made its way through the white wool.

'He was about to start home,' she said.

'Hearing Polly was free, eh?' inquired the Rector.

'I am sure I don't know if that was his reason. If it was, he will find letters at Bombay which will disabuse his mind 'of that idea. I have urged him, under the circumstances, to adhere to his original plan, to continue travelling with Mr. Quayle.'

'I'm afraid he won't obey you. If I know Lance, this last news will only make him come home the quicker.'

For a minute or two Mrs. Crookenden worked on silently at her crochet. Then she remarked, with truly alarming severity,—

'I must say Mary gives an immense amount of trouble to all who have the misfortune of being connected with her.'

The Rector's thin lips twitched and turned down oddly at one corner.

'That's been the way of pretty women from the beginning of history,' he said.

Mrs. Crookenden moved her mouth as though she had a bad taste in it. Sometimes she thought, she was sorry but she could not help it, that Kent was really rather coarse—but then after all there was a suspicion of that, you know, in all the Crookendens.

CHAPTER II.

THE summer was past. The leaves were falling. The fogs had begun. The Connop School had re-opened. Colthurst worked hard at this period. In addition to the regular routine of school work he had a large picture on the stocks, and a portrait of Mary Crookenden. The painting of this last gave him profound pleasure, intellectual as well as of the heart. He has put all his skill, all his love, all his divination of Mary's character into the painting of that picture. It remains a thing by itself. The public have had no opportunity of seeing it as yet ; when it is seen it must add solidly to Colthurst's reputation.

Yet he has not attempted to paint Miss Crookenden in what the majority of her admirers would have considered her best looks. For he went back on his old first impression of her. He has painted her pale, the brownish-red tinge almost suggestive of tears upon her eyelids and a solemnity in her beautiful eyes. He has painted the tired, troubled child whom he met years ago on the hillside, the fair, sad face which looked up at him out of the brown moorland pool; not the triumphant young beauty whose appearance society for some three or four seasons so relished. The snow is there, and that strange promise —to him so royally fulfilled of late—of fire beneath the snow ; but of Miss Crookenden as an exquisite and rather heartless taker of scalps there is, I am happy to say, no trace. Her moonlight beauty is sweet, pathetic, touched with a peculiar and subtle charm. In short, the portrait is great as the revelation of a nature—which, after all, is the highest way in which any portrait can be great.

But behind Colthurst's love, behind his work both private and public, still lay the unsolved problem of Jenny Parris. He had had no explanation with her ; intended to have none until his marriage was an accomplished fact. He meant to go to her then and tell her, as concisely as possible, that the thing was done. This was cruel, perhaps. But Colthurst did not care. To shield Mary was his increasing and solitary wish; and he watched over her with jealous care, knew all she did, everywhere she went, guarded her at every point, as he trusted, from unpleasant surprises, unpleasant hints. Meanwhile, to keep Jenny away from London was evidently desirable. Regularly every week during the past summer—for Colthurst was curiously methodical in some matters—he had forwarded her allowance via Captain Prust. Finally he wrote to her advising her wintering on the south coast for health's sake. He knew there would be a certain danger in making this suggestion. Ten to one it would have precisely the reverse effect to that he intended, Jenny having a pernicious disposition to do exactly what she was asked not to do. Still it was incumbent upon him to make the suggestion, both for her own and for safety's sake. Colthurst received no answer to his letter.

It point of fact, Jenny, after long hungering for some recognition, some sign from him beyond that inevitable weekly sum of money—which in her unreasoning, hot-headed way she had come to hate—finding his letter contained no tenderness, gave no hope of softening on his part, tore it up, in a passion of misery; and then, poor impulsive soul, sewed the fragments of it—as a sort of

amulet—into a corner of the piece of red flannel she wore
to protect her chest.   And further, she proceeded to pack
the paper-parcels, band-boxes, and sea-chest, notwithstanding Dot's tears and angry protests.   She must go
away, go back to Delamere Crescent; for there, at least, it
was possible to get at him, to send for him, if the worst
came to the worst.   With her usual luck, she lighted on a
streaming day for her journey, and caught a cold on the
Bishopstoke platform changing trains, which speedily
undid the good her long sojourn by the seaside had done
her.   .

So, by the middle of October, Jenny was back in her
old quarters again, Colthurst ignorant of the fact, she
ignorant of his changed prospects.   And thus things might
have remained, but for the gentleman connected with the
dramatic profession—the music-hall artist, in plain English
—who happened at this period to rent Mrs. Prust's drawing-
room floor.   For, returning in the small hours, his morning
sleep was a great consequence to the gentleman in
question; and that racking, straining cough of Jenny's in
the room immediately below—it usually came on badly
when she woke bathed in perspiration between four and
five o'clock—so disturbed his slumbers, that he had to
complain to Mrs. Prust.   The good woman, with a handsome
disregard of monetary considerations, took him up rather
short; informing him that there were plenty of other
apartments to let both ends of the Crescent, so if hers

didn't give satisfaction, he had best suit himself elsewhere.

'For,' she added, blinking and gurgling with emotion as she proceeded downstairs after the interview, 'the poor young thing shan't be drove out of this house, cough or no cough, as long as me and the Capt'n's above ground.'

Jenny's cough not mending, however, the gentleman belonging to the dramatic profession took Mrs. Prust at her word and sought another domicile. Mrs. Prust had the magnanimity not to disclose the cause of his abrupt departure; but, since the balance must be kept and excess of kindness in one direction of necessity begets defect in another, by a process of logic peculiar to herself she elected to hold Colthurst responsible for the loss of her lodger. She, therefore, once again, without consulting Jenny, despatched her reluctant master mariner to Wentworth Street in search of him, bearing a notification of Jenny's condition and a request 'that Mr. Colthurst would be pleased to lose no time in coming and looking into it all himself.'

But the message did not get itself delivered till next morning; for Colthurst was dining in St. George's Road. It was a very happy little dinner, the happier, perhaps, because Madame Jacobini had a headache which prevented her appearing until afterwards in the drawing-room. Colthurst was singularly brilliant that night; he had forgotten the great cat Fate and her random selection of victims. He talked his best, was full of energy, of schemes for coming pictures; his hesitating, urgent speech was unusually effective, varied, eloquent. Antony Hammond and Mr. Carr, who happened to come in for an hour during the course of the evening, both left under the spell of his wonderful force and vitality, left with the sense of having assisted at a rather superb exhibition of intellectual and artistic activity. Even Madame Jacobini was carried off her feet.

'Good heavens, my dear child,' she exclaimed, when he went away at last; 'but with the best will in the world to think otherwise, I must own that your Tartar is fascinating, when he pleases—absolutely fascinating. And it is not only his talk, for one has a conviction the creature will be as good as his word. He inspires one with a really marvellous confidence in his powers.'

Mary laughed. It appeared to her, also, that 'the creature' was magnificently capable, and that there was an ever new delight in loving and being loved by him.

But though—to make use once more of his own rather pagan illustration—though Colthurst might forget the great cat Fate, she had not forgotten him. Who, indeed, does she ever forget, if it comes to that? For while he dined with Miss Crookenden in St. George's Road, Captain Prust, arriving at the moment of the meal, sat down to supper with the landlady and her daughter in Wentworth Street. And the latter, as thank-offering for much nautical anecdote, supplied him with information of an extremely interesting character.—This would be about the last of his journeys here, they supposed, in search of Mr. Colthurst. Why didn't he—Captain Prust—know? And then followed the current gossip. An heiress—for Mr. Colthurst knew how to feather his own nest, it seemed—the lady's name, a decidedly exaggerated account of her wealth and position, and how she had come more than once in her own carriage to leave a note; her direction, too, but they weren't sure of the number.

As he went home with that rolling, sea-faring gait of his, Captain Prust took his pipe out of his mouth more than once, and exclaimed aloud :

'Lord love you, whatever will S'lome say? S'lome 'll raise a breeze will S'lome, and let him have it hot somehow.'

But someone with greater capacity—in the present case—for ' letting him have it hot ' than even Mrs. Prust, notwithstanding that good lady's gifts of state-ment, took this matter in hand. For the next after-noon, though there was a drizzling leaden-grey fog and though she had hardly been out of the house since her return, Jenny herself sallied forth. Dot teazed to go too, but her mother bade her stay at home in a tone which rather surprised that forth-coming and coer-cive little person. First Jenny visited the newsagent, who kept the post-office two streets off, and with his assistance made out a certain address from the directory. Then she went away slowly through the chill of the dreary late autumn day, holding the fur shoulder-cape, she wore over her claret-coloured ulster, together across her aching chest ; breathing with difficulty in the thick atmosphere, stopping now and again to fight down a fit of coughing ; yet carrying her head erect, moving with some of her old, statuesque grace, supported by the terrible purpose she had at heart. Several times she lost herself, for the fog grew denser as the afternoon advanced, and it was not easy to read the names of the streets—overshot the turning she wanted, made her way back again, found the house at last.

Jenny stood on the pavement looking up at it. A soft glow came through the lace curtains of the drawing-room windows ; even from the outside it had an effect of luxury which bitterly incensed her. She leaned against the right-hand pillar of the portico to recover her breath. The clammy cold of the fog wrapped her round like a wet sheet, until she shivered ; yet the stifling, choking pain at her chest made her long for more air, not less. For respiration is hardly comfortable work when you have spit up the larger half of one lung and the vessels of the other are clogged by matter and blood.

As she waited in the heavy leaden greyness, a brougham drove up, and almost immediately the house door opened disclosing a perspective of warm colour and subdued light within. A young lady came the length of the hall, out on to the steps, and then turned to give some message to the maid holding open the door. Jenny had a full view of her. She saw a woman, tall, richly dressed, mistress of herself, and perfectly finished from head to heel as only women of the leisured classes can be—have time and money to be. Saw a lovely face, with a sort of lofty gladness in its expression, as of one who carries store of some great happiness constantly about with her. For the moment she was almost awed, almost moved to pity; this woman was so young, so serene, so very fair. But jealousy such as Jenny's knows neither fear or mercy for long. From the first she did not question Mary's identity; and the contrast between herself, ill, worn, wretched, spoilt, standing on the greasy pavement, and this exquisite child of good fortune, was too glaring. It infuriated Jenny, it inspired her with the daring and the dignity of intolerable wrong. She shook back her head, swept forward, stood at the bottom of the steps, the light from the open hall door falling upon her. She looked full, aggressively at Mary, as the latter prepared to descend the steps.

' You'm Miss Crookenden ? ' she said.

The young lady, startled, slightly annoyed, bowed a sufficiently haughty assent.

' Then I'm bound to speak to you,' Jenny added.

This handsome, battered woman, her appearance at once showy and shabby, her bearing almost insolent, her manner almost authoritative, was displeasing to Miss Crookenden from every point of view.

' I think you are under some mistake,' she replied. ' I am not aware that I know you.'

' No, you don't know me, and that's just where it is,' Jenny returned. ' You'm bound to know me, to know all about me.'

Mary tried to retain her cold indifference of manner, but the incident was unexpected to the point of embarrassment and she spoke with a certain haste.

' I cannot stay to hear what you may have to say now. I have an engagement. As you see, the carriage is waiting. I am going out. And I have no idea on what subject you can possibly require to speak to me.'

Jenny came up two steps, came close to her.

' I want to speak to you about the man you'm going to marry—about James Colthurst,' she said.

An indeterminate, vague horror seemed to pass before Mary Crookenden.

' I do not discuss Mr. Colthurst with strangers,' she replied.

' I'm no stranger,' Jenny said, contemptuously. ' Jim and me have been pretty intimate for a sight of years now.'

And then, in obedience to one of those swift changes of feeling which made her at once so impossible and—in a way—so fine, Jenny, seeing the growing fear in the young face before her, spoke indulgently, as one speaks to a child.

' There, I don't want to hurt you more'n I can help,'
she said. ' And it ain't fit for such as you to be standing
here talking to me in the street. You'm bound to hear it
all sooner or later, best get it over at once. Send away
your carriage, and let me come inside.'

Swallowing the cold, damp air as she talked provoked
Jenny's cough. She leaned one hand on the balustrade of
the portico now for support, for the exertion of coughing
doubled her together and made her unsteady on her feet.

'It'll pass,' she gasped, ' after a bit. Only let me come
inside. I won't keep you longer than I must.—It'll be pretty
rough on both of us—but let me come in. The fog's
killing and I am awful tired. Let me rest a bit.'

Mary Crookenden debated ; and then, moved by the
sight of the woman's sad condition, moved by that indeterminate horror—to which any certainty, however damaging,
seemed preferable—making a sign to Jenny to follow,
turned and went into the house.

' If anyone calls I am engaged,' she said to the amazed
and discreetly blank-faced Hannah. ' Remember I see no
one until I ring. The carriage can go back to the stables ;
if I want it I will send round later.'

She led the way into the dining-room. The shaded
lamp hanging over the dinner table was already lighted,
and the table laid for three. Colthurst dined with the two
ladies again to-night, dined early, as they proposed going
to the theatre. Her own picture looked at Mary with an

odd fixedness — so it seemed—from its casel in a shadowy
corner of the charming, tasteful room. She stood just out of
the circle of light cast by the lamp. She pulled off her
gloves, locked her hands together, her attitude strained,
her face unresponsive, set like a mask.

'You had better sit down,' she said, 'since you are
tired. And please oblige me by telling me what you wish
to tell me briefly and at once.'

Jenny took the nearest chair, perforce, for she had not
strength to stand and talk both. It happened to be the
one set at the table for Colthurst. Mary bit her lip. It was
all she could do to prevent crying out.—Then Jenny
glanced round the room deliberately; glanced at the portrait
in the shadowy corner, at the silver, the dainty glass, the
dessert and heaped up flowers upon the dinner table,
finally fastened her eyes upon the girl herself.

'Jim knows well enough what he's about as usual,' she
said; and her jealousy, her sense of the immense contrast
between her own lot and that of her companion, became
well nigh insupportable. She leaned back in her chair,
resting both wrists on the table, and stated her case against
Colthurst baldly, mercilessly, without gradation, without
those extenuating circumstances which put so wholly different a complexion upon some phases at all events of her
miserable history. But jealousy and envy raised the devil
in poor Jenny Parris. She struck and struck again, caring
nothing how or where she struck so long as she drew blood.

' You want to have it short—very well, then, here it is. My name's Jane Parris. I come from Beera Mills, over right Brattleworthy, where you Crookenden folks live. Jim painted me there, made me love him there, a dozen years ago. And Jim's like that, once care for him you can't get along without him. I couldn't stay when he was gone. I came up after him here to London.'

The red showed in a hard triangle on either of Jenny's hollow cheeks.

' You want to have it,' she repeated, flinging the short, gasping sentences at Mary Crookenden, with a growing violence. ' Well, then, listen here. He's kept me ever since, except when I've kept him. I've a child he's the father of. He keeps us still.'

And the sentences hit Mary Crookenden blow on blow till her imagination positively rocked under them. Still she managed to maintain a show of outward calm.

' You make these dreadful assertions, but you bring no proof,' she said, proudly. ' I have nothing beyond your bare word for their truth. Till I have more than that I shall not believe them.'

Yet even while she spoke Mary's mind misgave her. All Colthurst's allusions to a shame and wretchedness in his life, his old declaration that his love was hopeless, his later attempts to tell her that which she persistently refused to hear, Lancelot's hinted story—all these crowded into her mind, giving the woman's statements a distressing air of probability.

' If you don't believe me, ask Jim then,' Jenny replied. ' Jim's cruel hard by times, but I've never known him lie. He won't deny me and the child; I don't think that of him.   And Cap'n and Mrs. Prust know all about it.   And, if you want proofs, I've got letters and things of his down to our place.   And if you want more, well, there's the child —if you don't believe me, I reckon you've only to look a bit at Dot.'

In her increasing excitement Jenny pulled off her hat, threw it down on the carpet beside her and with her left hand impatiently rubbed back the masses of her dark hair.   She was very terrible just then in her coarsened beauty, her untidy attire, her broken health, her great sense of wrong.   Mary saw her face clearly for the first time ; saw it and alas! knew it, wasted by disease, disfigured by passion though it was, for the face of the woman in Colthurst's great picture, the face of the woman of Slerracombe deer-park, and knowing it turned sick as death.

·   ' Have you done ?' she said.   ' Because if so, go—go at once.'

Jenny swept the glasses, the fish knife and fork to left and right, pushed the basket-folded napkin back against the flowers, obliterated the place laid for Colthurst—for the man she loved, the man whom, in obedience to that love (so queerly does human affection display itself) she was now seeking to blast and dishonour—forgetting all his patience towards her, forgetting too—and let us not forget it, for sentiment in these lamentable cases is very much too prone to run amuck at the man, and range itself wholly and blindly on the side of the woman—forgetting that in the first instance she was at least as much to blame as he was, as much tempter as tempted, as ready to seduce as to yield to seduction. Then she rested her elbows on the table, her chin in both hands, and gazed fixedly once more at Miss Crookenden.

'No, I've not done yet,' she answered. 'For he's mine, he's mine by right, mine before Almighty God. Times and again he promised he'd marry me. And so I swore I'd come and tell you.'

'And you have told me,' Mary said. 'Now go.'

'But will you give him up?' Jenny demanded.

For a long minute the two looked across the dinner-table into each other's eyes.

'Till I know more, no,' Mary Crookenden said.

'Ah! you're a brave one,' Jenny cried. Then she settled her chin in her hands again.—'All the same he's mine, I tell you. What'll you do for him against what I've done? Will you wash and mend and cook for him, stretch his canvasses, clean his palettes, stand for him the livelong day in your clothes and out of them?'

Mary made a movement of haughty repudiation. Jenny tossed back her head, and her voice, husky from that ailing throat and chest, grew fuller, deeper, with sheer force of defiant emotion.

' I've done that, and more than that,' she went on. ' When he was ill and times were bad, I've worked for him.   I've stood model in all the studios worth naming in London, and Paris too for that matter.   And the painters have been rarely pleased to get me, for I've had my share of good looks as well as the rest.—And I've done more'n that.   Four years ago when he was took so ill it was summer time, and the schools were shut and most everyone was holiday-making, so trade was awful slack.'

Jenny paused, lowered her eyes, began playing nervously with Colthurst's fish knife and fork.

' But there's one trade at which a healthy woman can always make a living in a big town, worse luck.   And Jim was awful bad.   It was touch and go with him.   We hadn't a brass farthing left.'

Her head went down into her hands, her shoulders heaved and shook.

' And Jim's not the man you'll let die if there's a way to help it.   He's worth a sight too much.   So I took to that trade.   To keep him and the child alive I walked the cursed hell of those Paris streets.'

On those last words a long silence followed.   Mary Crookenden stood perfectly still, a great sense of disgrace upon her, making her whole body burn and tingle from head to foot.   For the gross bestial side of existence, the smallest hint of which all her life long she had so studiously and proudly ignored, from which she had turned so loftily away, suddenly lay bare and open before her.   The corruption which runs below the seemly surface of our every-day life, even as sewers below some majestic city, the corruption which is a constant quantity in human nature, civilized and savage alike, suddenly sent up its stench into her nostrils. And so, just now, it was not her private grief, not the question of Colthurst's wrong-doing, his guilt or innocence in respect of this unhappy woman, not the question of his future relation to herself, which so appalled Mary Crookenden; rather was it this uncompromising revelation of the evil—ah! the infinite pity of it!—indissolubly joined, as beast with god, to that apparently best and dearest gift bestowed on mortals, the gift of love.

'The Lord'll forgive me,' Jenny murmured hoarsely, at last.   'I reckon He will, but I doubt Jim won't never forgive.   Jim can't forget it.   He always goes back on it. He's been changed to me ever since.'

After a while she raised her head, got on to her feet. Pushed back her hair languidly, tried to pin on her hat ; but now that her passion was spent she felt her weakness doubly.   The room turned with her, she was giddy and faint.

' I'll go.   I've told you pretty well all, as I swore I'd tell any of you fine ladies who he might want to marry.   Now you know how it stands between him and me.'

Jenny lurched, laid hold of the back of the chair, sat down again.

'I'll go,' she repeated. 'But I feel mortal bad. I'm parched.'

A cut glass jug of iced water was standing on the table near her. She put out her hand, tried to raise it ; but her wrist gave, the ice rattled and the water slopped over on to the cloth.—'Ah ! dear heart,' Jenny exclaimed.

Then Mary Crookenden recovered herself, and putting a great force upon herself, came round from the further side of the table, took the claret glass that had been set for Colthurst, filled it with water, placed a dessert dish before the woman full of grapes.

' Eat—drink,' she said.

So far Jenny had thought only of herself, had acted under the dominion of her sense of injury alone. But the tone of Miss Crookenden's grave voice, the graciousness of her action, stirred the nobler spirit in poor Jenny. And as she looked up at the girl, and saw the proudly glad face of less than an hour ago cruelly altered, rigid and ghastly as that of a corpse, she understood something of the immense suffering she had inflicted, repented, was overcome by remorse.

' No, no,' she said, pushing away the grapes. ' I'll go —I must go. I'm not so bad but what I can walk, and it's not fitting I should eat or drink in this house.'

She rose, went through the warm, bright hall, opened the street door. Then she gave a great cry, for there against the blurred, shifting, mournful dimness of the fog was Colthurst's tall, high-shouldered figure.

' Ah ! you are here, you've seen her, you have taken your revenge at last. D-damn you, damn you, d-damn you, Jenny Parris,' he said.

CHAPTER III.

AT sea it was a wild night, and on land it was not much better. The half-dozen small slate-roofed houses that cluster about the four roads at Beera Cross were shut up, only a square of redness here and there, through a curtain tight-strained behind the flower-pots, across their little windows. The Brattleworthy carrier's van stops to set down passengers, on its way back from Yeomouth, three times a week at the Cross about eight o'clock. And Jenny Parris staggered, as she stepped out of that close-packed, jolting, rattling vehicle.

This was one of her impulsive escapades, one of her mad revolts against circumstance and conditions. All other comfort failing, her heart had turned in unreasoning desire towards her own people, her own country. It had seemed to her that once down in the West all would be changed, health and beauty would come back ; for poor Jenny was incurably hopeful even at this pass. And so, not as repentant prodigal but as seeker after her lost youth, she had left Delamere Crescent that morning, left kindly Mrs. Prust tearful, shaking her head. And as the train brought her further and further westward, as the soft air caressed her cheek, the fine-featured, high-coloured, West country folk met her eye, the glib familiar speech met her ear, Jenny's spirits rose. She had felt unusually well to-day, the dragging weight of illness had become less burdensome.—Dave would be good to her, father would be good to her. The path of life, which for so long now had run persistently downhill, would turn, begin to ascend disclosing pleasant prospects. She longed, with a foolish, unreasoning, heart-sick longing, for the smell of the sea, longed to handle the herring nets, longed to hear the trample and grind of the ground-swell on the beach. It seemed to her, as I say, she might recover thus her lost youth; and recovering that, might even yet recover her lost love. Colthurst might return to her, return forgetting much that had fallen out but ill of late, forgetting the terrible words he had spoken, forgetting all —as she just now was so willing to forget—save that once, long ago, here in the tender-hearted West country she and he had courted and loved.

This sounds absurd; but the Celt is always absurd, extravagant, impossible. Of them it is written, 'They went forth to the war, but they always fell.' Written truly—romantic, wrong-headed, infinitely pathetic race! And now, at this lowest ebb of her fortunes, the irrepressible Celt arose in Jenny, making her sing a swan-song of longing, of foolish, baseless hope. If she went away from London, went away to the home of her girl-hood, she would find her girlhood there, awaiting her.

But the swan-song had died down, somewhat, during those jolting nine miles out from Yeomouth; died down yet lower as she stood now in the open space before the small, close-shut cottages at Beera Cross, while the carrier's van rattled and bumped away into the distance along the straight, high-banked Roman road. For there was still a good mile to walk, and the night, though warm, was wild; and the westerly wind, though soft as milk, was boisterous. It drove shouting over the bare upland country, broke in great waves against the little huddled houses, roared through the oak, beech and larch woods where it struck them in the windings of the combe. The moon was past the full, a low-hanging, stormy moon, blurred and irregular in outline, and encircled by a great reddish halo; a moon showing fitfully between the floats of dark ragged cloud, that raced up out of the Atlantic across the pallid grey-green sky and across her face.

Jenny had not reckoned with accessories of storm and darkness when she set forth'; had not reckoned seriously with the fact that she knew practically nothing of what awaited her at Beera, did not know, indeed, whether her father was yet alive or not. In starting on this wild-goose chase her mind, according to its fatal custom, had

overstepped intervening difficulties and grasped merely at
the fancied end to be reached.   But now alone, save for
Dot,—bewildered and sleepy, clinging in most unwonted
spirit of dependence close against her,—face to face with
the tumult of the night, poor Jenny's swan-song died down,
and the intervening difficulties took on large propor-
tions.   She dreaded the long walk down the combe ; the
van was gone, however, and a shyness possessed her, she
could not make up her mind to knock at those closed doors
and ask for a night's shelter or even for a lantern, so she
turned down the steep lane which seemed to yawn a dark
abyss ahead.

Dot hung back.   The London-bred child, at home in the
streets, fearless before that most alarming of all phenomena
to some of us, a human crowd, shrunk from this close-
ness to nature.

'Oh ! I'm awful scared to go down into that ugly old
black place, Mammy,' she whispered.

Jenny was half scared herself.   But there was no help
for it.   So she kept tight hold of the child's hand.

'Don't be a silly,' she said.   'There's nothing to harm
you.   We'm going home.'

And so hugging the left bank for shelter, stumbling in the
deep, moist wheel-tracks by the roadside, they struggled on.

At the turn of the combe the little church, nestled in
the hillside, rose sharply defined against the gloom of
woods beyond.   And the grave-stones stood up white and

stark, seeming to move, sway, incline towards each other in ghostly confabulation as the cloud shadows rushed over them. Then Jenny, superstitious as she was, became scared in truth. And though her breath was short, her knees weak, she hurried the child on down the hill, gasping, not daring to look behind her. For in the cry and swish of the wind, in the rustle of fallen oak and beech leaves whirling along the road-way beside her, she heard the stifled, pleading voices of the dead—mother, friends of long ago, a baby sister whom she had lost as little more than a baby herself, poor nameless corpses, too, cast up maimed and disfigured by the ocean along that iron coast—calling to her to come and join them, to lie beside them in their shallow, rock-floored graves. Her pace quickened almost to a run. The swan-song of hope died out completely in her heart; and Dot fell to sobbing, mingling her pitiful little private and personal out-cry with the thousand-tongued lament of the gale in the woods.

Here the road narrows, is more closed in and overhung by trees. A heavy cloud obscured the moon too, making the darkness for some hundred yards profound. And poor Dot sobbed and slipped, slipped and .sobbed. She had on a smart little pair of new yellow boots, high-heeled, smooth-soled, a present from Captain Prust, as ill-suited as boots could well be to the alternately rocky and slimy road—for, thanks to the large amount of rain which had fallen of late, springs had broken up right in the middle of

M 2

it, washing the road-metal bare in places and in others forming long streaks of rusty, iron-stained mud. Fortunately the wind lessened, there was a partial lull, the tumult of sound abated. Jenny walked slower. She felt as though she had a band across her chest that was being drawn ever tighter and tighter till the pain of it amounted to agony, and her mouth filled—she knew the taste only too well—filled with blood.

Just then the moon sailed out from behind the cloud and spread a tender sorrowful-seeming light over the road, the woods, and the steep hillsides. And immediately on her right, weird, mystic, fairy-like under that thin, silvery radiance, Jenny saw the rough cart-track buried in large-leaved butter-burr, leading up through the larch plantation to the disused stone-quarry; the gate, the little bridge of slate slabs spanning the stream. It was here she and Colthurst had given and taken their first fatal kiss, and so the spot was dear and dreadful to her both at once.

Still, though she wiped it away again and again, the blood rose in her throat, stained her lips. She had never bled like this before; and a sombre belief settled down on Jenny that at this rate the voices calling from the church-yard would not call long in vain; that not health and recovered girlhood but something very different awaited her in the little white-walled town that weary half-mile below. And the settling down of this belief was very frightful to her. With the giving-out of hope came a giving-out of physical strength. She was too distressed, too disheartened, for the moment, to go further. She crossed the rough bridge, sank down among the lush damp growth of grass and ferns, leaned her poor head against the gate-post. While Dot, throwing her arms about her mother's waist, hiding her face in her lap, cried aloud—partly in panic terror of the storm, the loneliness, the large mystery of the night, partly in childish misery over the soiling and spoiling by mud and wet of her smart, new, yellow boots.

'I wants to go back, Mammy. I wants to go back to the Capt'n and Mrs. Prust,' she wailed. 'It's awful ugly here with nothing but trees and no streets. Why ever don't they light the gas? And I'm ever so hungry, and there's cold creepy-crawlies running up my legs. And the moon's nasty, all crooked like it's got a swelled face. Oh! Mammy, let's go back. I won't never call it poky again if you'll only go back.'

But as the blood rose, hot, acrid, nauseous into her mouth, the conviction deepened in Jenny that she should never go back. Yet it was not so much the fear of death as an immense, profound, all-engulfing regret for the false promises of life which caused her most poignant grief. Pushing the crying child away with an incontrollable movement of impatience, she flung the skirt of her gown up over her face and head, and thus veiled, rocked herself to and fro in the frail moonlight, and wept and wept.

CHAPTER IV.

ON the window-seat in the Rector's study among an orderly confusion of piled up pamphlets, transactions of learned societies in drab and blue covers, and miscellaneous *disjecta membra* of printed matter, Mary Crookenden sat waiting for the post to come in. The Rector's study, though uncompromisingly square, is a pleasant room, lined on three sides with book-shelves from floor to ceiling. Its furnishings are by no means new, but they have a certain friendly comfortableness about them from long use. Mary could remember the room just as it now was, since the early years of her childhood. Neither it or Uncle Kent ever changed. The firelight danced over the big tiger-skin rug and the deep crimson-covered arm-chairs just as cosily, and Kent Crookenden's steady, kindly eyes met hers just as reassuringly now as when she wore those very short and staring-coloured frocks which had so disturbed Mrs. Crookenden's sense of propriety.

Out of doors the three days' gale was abating at last; but the wind still blew gusty, driving the fine, soft rain past the window in silver-grey scuds. The heart-shaped lawn and carriage-sweep were strewn with leaves, the rusty reds and browns of which offered a sharp contrast to the vivid green of the turf and purple-blue tones of the shingly gravel. The said carriage-sweep is bordered by a thick-set shrubbery of rhododendron under a ring of trees; the upper branches of which, bared by the gale, framed in an irregular oval of grey sky, while between the trunks of them looking away to the front gate past the stables, was a vagueness of hurrying mist.

Nature still quivered, as it seemed, from the recent violence of storm and tempest. The outlook was a melancholy one; but Mary liked it none the less well for that. She felt grateful, indeed, to the Earth-Mother for setting her great symphony in a minor key, and fingering out only low-toned pensive music. For over the girl, like-wise, a tempest had passed, from which she still quivered, from which her inward sky was still overcast. The shock of her interview with James Colthurst's former mistress had been profound, had shaken the very foundations of her being. It had wounded her pride; wounded her moral sense; had endangered her trust in herself and in those innate beliefs which had so far ruled her conduct; it had changed all the values; put a new complexion on much she had learned of late to hold dearest. It had effected nothing less, indeed, than a revolution in her outlook on life. Finally, it had raised a practical question of the very gravest moment; a question which it was impossible to ignore, which she was compelled to answer. Not that her affection for Colthurst was lessened. It remained; its dominion over her was strong as ever. But the quality of it had suffered change. It had lost its brilliancy, lost its fearless delight, above all, had lost its innocence. For during her interview with Jenny Parris she had been forced, willy-nilly, to eat of the fruit of the tree of the knowledge of good and evil, and to her sorrow, to her shame—a shame, the bitterness of which no man, I fancy, will ever quite understand or measure—her eyes were opened. She recoiled with the anger, with the fierce disdain, that is a constant quantity in the purity of a noble young girl.

And under the influence of that recoil she too had turned her steps westward. She required to be alone, required to think. Required to adjust her mind to the altered aspect that this bitter increase of knowledge gave to life. Required, above all, to find an answer to that practical question of right and wrong, the answering of which—for she did not permit herself to blink the truth—involved not only her own future, but that of three other persons as well.

The fundamental rectitude of Mary's nature displayed itself rather admirably at this juncture. Cost her what it might, until that question was answered, she had told herself she would not see James Colthurst again.

Happily Slerracombe House was empty, Mrs. Crookenden and Carrie having gone up to London to welcome the Duckingfields back from their wedding-tour, and assist in inducting them to the large and somewhat funereal mansion they had elected to take in Cromwell Road. So Brattleworthy offered a safe harbour of refuge, as it appeared to our storm-tost maiden, where she might think the sad thoughts born of deepening experience and arrive at right conclusions in peace.

Cyprian Aldham, it is true, was still at Beera, for he had turned back in a sternly ascetic spirit to undiluted clerical-ism and parochialism on the breaking off of his marriage. The sacerdotal note was the master-note, after all, in Mr. Aldham. But then it appeared probable to Mary that Aldham would dislike meeting her, at least as much as she would dislike meeting him; so that she did not think it necessary to let his neighbourhood deter her from going to Brattleworthy. She wanted quiet, she wanted the support of an unbiassed judgment; and that support, when she had sufficient fortitude to tell her grief and ask for it, she believed, and rightly, she would get from her uncle, the Rector.

The post came in extra late, as it invariably does when one sits at the window wishing and watching. But it came at last, and Mary received her letters.

One from dear faithful Sara Jacobini, that was a matter of course. One with Indian stamps and post-marks. Mary sighed, laid it in her lap unopened.—What poor Lance had to say would keep; it could not be gay reading, particularly just now. But there was a third letter, to which Mary's fingers clung very tenderly as she handled it, while her eyebrows drew together and her lips grew white.

'How can I reason with you?' Colthurst wrote.
'You have flown off at a tangent. You forget that
nothing is really altered in our relation to one
another. I am substantially the same person, you substantially the same likewise. The past days are just as
sacred, the coming days may be just as sweet as ever
we dreamed before you knew this thing. And see,
it was always there—there no more, but equally, there
no less, now that you know of its existence. It has
become not one bit more real, more actual, more potent
for evil, by the fact of your having knowledge of it.
Therefore, be reasonable, my best beloved. Don't mistake shadow for substance; regard the thing simply—in
an unexaggerated light. Do not allow sentiment to warp
your judgment.'

If this trenched on sophistry, to Mary it was sophistry
of a dangerously coercive sort. For as she read she
could hear Colthurst's voice, broken, by emotion, urgent,
yet gentle, pleading with her in every sentence. Could
feel the strange charm alike of his power and his weakness; the upsetting pathos of the man's tremendous personality combined with his childlike trust and dependence
on herself. Ah! it was splendid after all to be loved by
James Colthurst.

Instinctively she shifted her position a little, raised her
head, her eyes began to dilate, her lips to regain their
colour. And as she moved, Lancelot's unopened letter

fetched way, slipped off her lap, lodged in a cleft between the Anthropological Society's reports and the transactions of the British Association for 18—. Mary paid no heed to it; after a minute's pause she read on.

'And see, my darling, at least I have done you no wrong. Long before I met you last summer, I had parted, to all intents and purposes, with Jenny Parris. Years ago she pleased the baser part of me—but, it is a profanation to speak of the affection I once bore her and that which I bear you, on the same page. Women such as you have but one sort of love to give, holy, undefiled, complete. We men, alas, have many sorts of love to give, so you must not judge us by your standard. Nature perhaps, custom and habit certainly, have made us grievously different in this respect. Only understand that whatever quality of love I may have entertained for her is dead long ago. She herself, by her own action, destroyed it. Still I have no desire to go into that, to clear myself at her expense, or to use her offences as a cloak for my own. I will deal justly by her—don't be afraid. She shall not want and her child shall be provided for. But from henceforth she passes out of our lives—yours and mine. I will arrange all that. And yet, though it sounds like a paradox, I am almost thankful she declared herself to you, for now no shadow of concealment is between us. You know, I tried to tell you, but you would not hear. Believe me, if you can forgive the passing distress, that this has happened is best for us both—if you will only be reasonable.'

Mary leaned her head against the window sash, and gazed out at the wind and wet. It was not easy to resist that pleading voice; while easy enough, in response to its pleading, to be reasonable according to the fashion it enjoined.

'And so by the memory of all our best hours together, by the memory of every promise, every gracious word, every caress—in the name of the redemption you have worked in me, in my thoughts, ambitions, purposes—I implore you to put away the remembrance of this vile thing, in as far as it comes between us, cuts you off from me, keeps us apart. Because, my dearest, if you do not I cannot answer for myself. I used to be pretty well able to face the world alone. I can't do so any longer. Without you the clue is lost, I have nothing to guide me, nothing to steer by. The last three days have been infernal. I dare not write, hardly dare think about them. They have been days of outer darkness. I fancied I knew what torment was, but it seems I did not. This was something new. I have no words for it—it was the abomination of desolation. For a while even Art herself was false to me, turned grotesque; mocked me, drawing aside her garments and showing me that under the goodly seeming of them was nothingness, vacancy, a strong delusion. Mary, no man has ever loved a woman more devoutly than I you. I

must have you. By God, I will have you. See, across
the distance you have put between us, I stretch out my
arms to you. Dear love, you won't have the heart to
resist—you will hear, understand the greatness of my need,
yield, forget. Already I hold you, see your eyes again,
kiss your lips—then all is well. Short of that, oh, well,
short of that—for loving as I love you no less than that,
no compromise, is possible—for me there remains only the
abomination of desolation. So give way, my dear one—
hear me, and forget.'

Shall we condemn Mary Crookenden as light-minded,
wanting in strength of purpose, of moral stamina, because, by the time she had finished reading Colthurst's
letter, heart had gained over head, because she ceased
struggling to discriminate between abstract right and
wrong in an all-compelling awareness of her lover's
desperate need of her ; because, in short, the great god
once more conquered, came into possession of his own
again ? Human nature being what it is, and we ourselves,
excellent reader, being after all, you know, but human,
had best perhaps be silent, cover our mouth.

Getting up, clasping her hands behind her, the letter
in them, she began walking backwards and forwards
across the room; first the warm firelight, then, as she
turned, the wan, pensive light of the autumn morning
alternately touching her figure.

' Yes, I will give way,' she answered, out loud. ' I
understand. I will try to forget.'

And then, once having yielded, the longing to relieve his suspense, to shorten the time of his probation, took possession of Mary Crookenden. She went back to the window—if it was not too wet she would go out now quickly, by herself, go up to the post-office in the village, telegraph to him at once.

But though the rain was not heavy, Mary left the window hastily, in consternation, for, walking up the carriage-drive, his long black mackintosh shiny from the damp, was no less a person than Mr. Aldham himself. And the sight of him, at this particular moment, was particularly jarring to Miss Crookenden. To cross the hall with a view to going upstairs, she must pass the front door, so it appeared safer to stay where she was. Fortunately the Rector was out. But Aldham's near neighbourhood made her extremely nervous, all the same; for it brought keenly before her the most unsatisfactory episode in her experience. On the face of it she had behaved badly to Mr. Aldham, had made a fool of him. He was not precisely the kind of person who relishes being made a fool of; and on parting with her he had permitted himself to tell her quite plainly his opinion of her behaviour. His remarks had been extremely pungent. Mary reddened at the mere recollection of them. The events of the last week had been sad enough, heaven knows, but they at least had been dignified; and there was something very distasteful, displeasing to her in having these other inglorious recollections—not only of Mr. Aldham's speeches, but of all the strife of tongues that had arisen around her broken engagement, and of all that odious business of returning her wedding presents—revived just now. It seemed to vulgarize the present, to cheapen it. Mary stood on the tiger-skin rug, full of resentment, her hands behind her still clasping Colthurst's letter.

In the long run, I suppose, we all really do what we like best; and on that hypothesis, Mr. Aldham unquestionably liked doing what more malleable and less rigidly self-opiniated persons would have voted highly embarrassing and disagreeable. For after a very short delay, the study door was opened and the servant ushered him into the room.

Aldham had preserved the gift of extracting all personal and related meaning from his expression, and presenting himself to you as a chilly abstraction. He might have been meeting Miss Crookenden for the first time. The effect was neither pleasant or reassuring. He bowed on entering the room, came within speaking distance, delivered himself of his business deliberately, with unbending severity of manner.

'I find Mr. Crookenden is out,' he said. 'I therefore think it best to speak directly to you. This will save time, and in the present case time is of importance. I come in the interests of one of my parishioners.'

Mary inclined her head in acknowledgment of this speech. If he was cold, she at least could be cold too—all the same her cheeks were burning. The position appeared to her singularly ungraceful.

'I was called in early this morning to a woman who, apparently, is dying. She informs me that you are acquainted with her and with her unfortunate career. She is most desirous to see you, as she has something to communicate to you which—so she says—it is impossible for her to mention to any but yourself. She has been away from Beera for many years. She is a daughter, I learn, of the Dissenting lobster-catcher, William Parris.'

Mary could not help herself—it hurt too much—she gave a sort of imploring cry. The severity of Aldham's bearing suffered no diminution. His lips were tightly compressed, his light blue eyes as hard as steel. He told himself he was acting rightly, acting as the priest is bound to act, letting no private considerations interfere with the duty he owes to a member of his flock. He told himself he suffered acutely. He did not add that revenge is sweet. It took Mary some moments to recover herself, during that time he waited silent.

'You have alluded to—to this woman's unfortunate career,' the girl said at last, in proud desperation. 'Do you know what it has been?'

'In part, yes,' Aldham answered calmly.

'Then surely you must see, you must understand that

I cannot hold any communication with her. To ask me to do so is to insult me, Mr. Aldham.'

The young clergyman's delicate face grew scarlet, but he retained self-possession.

'That, pardon me, is beside the mark,' he replied. 'This unfortunate woman, Jane Parris, is in very poor circumstances, deserted by the person upon whom she has the strongest claim, she is mortally ill. Her case is a lamentable one ; and I, as her pastor, am under the obligation, at whatever cost to myself, to do what I can to mitigate her suffering. She entreats to see you, Miss Crookenden ; and I own it appears to me, that far from its being impossible you should accede to her request, she has a peculiar right to your consideration. Since she has expressed the wish, expressed it most earnestly I may add, I do not myself comprehend how you can conscientiously refuse to gratify it.'

Again Aldham waited silently, while in Mary Crookenden a rather agonizing battle went forward. For it was cruel, cruel, surely, that just now when her whole spirit was molten, so to speak, by the passion of those concluding sentences of Colthurst's letter, she should be called to perform this tremendous act of self-abnegation. She began to walk up and down again, her head bent, her eyes fixed upon the ground, the room very still save for the dragging rustle of her gown, the crackle of the fire, the swish of the rain against the window.

And Aldham, not without an unconscious but very actual

satisfaction, watched her, registering the progress of the battle.   Depend upon it, the view of human nature which sees in Inquisitors nothing but monsters of brutality and iniquity is an uncommonly crude one.   Most acting members of the Holy Office, I fancy, were extremely fine gentlemen whose intellectual and moral sense was exquisitely well-trained.

At length the girl stopped ; and Aldham had to own that the stately quality of her beauty had never been more notable than in this moment of humiliation and defeat.

' Please tell Jane Parris she may expect me this afternoon—that is, if it is not inconvenient to you to give her a message,' she said.

' Not in the least.   But I should fail in discharging my mission unless I stated that she expresses the greatest anxiety to see you some time before to-day's post goes out.'

Then Mary began to gauge the greatness of the sacrifice that would be demanded of her.   She flinched, would have prayed for mercy, perhaps, had any one but Cyprian Aldham been the bearer of this call upon her courage.   As it was she answered him calmly.

' In that case I need not trouble you with any message. I will order the carriage at once, and shall reach Beera sooner than you will.'

She went towards the door, Aldham moved too, opened it, held it open for her.   Mary bowed as she passed, but without looking at him. And Aldham told himself once more he had suffered acutely during this conversation.

'But I did right in speaking, in not sparing myself,' he added. 'I did quite right.'

And later that same morning, Mary Crookenden, the purest, most gracious instincts of her womanhood called forth by the irresistible appeal of poverty, sickness, the on-coming of the mystery of death, knelt on the uneven, worm-eaten floor beside Jenny's testerless bed, listened to her husky, gasping speech and answered her very gently.

'I thought on the grapes and the glass of water,' Jenny said, 'I knew you were like that, when you heard how bad I was you'd come. There's not many of your sort as 'ud do it, but I reckoned you would, because of that glass of water.'

'Yes,' Mary murmured, soothingly; 'yes.'

'Dying's a poor enough tale, anyway,' Jenny went on; 'but it's most past bearing, when you have to go all alone, with the curse on you of the one you've loved best. I know I ought to set my thoughts on the Lord, and so I do. But somehow your heart turns back, spite of you. And Jim's very strong—nothing don't frighten you much when he's by. You know all about that.'

'Yes,' Mary Crookenden murmured again. 'Ah, yes.'

'Poor, dear soul,' Jenny gasped. 'It's pretty rough on you, too. But you'll make him forgive me? You'll let me see him again, for certain?'

And once more Mary assented. Then Jenny raised herself a little, spoke with a tremulous haste.

'Only you'll make him understand he's bound to come on the quiet, when father's out to sea, because he's mad against Jim for the scandal he holds he's brought on the place along of me. Aunt Sarah Jane is always tellin' what he says he'll do to him if he ever shows his face in Beera town.'

Jenny sank back upon her poor pillows.

'And God knows, I'd rather go unforgiven, sooner go without ever setting eyes on him again, though it 'ud be awful hard, than that any harm should overtake him.'

Jenny smiled a little to herself.

'Jim's too good to waste,' she said.

But that smile touched the limit of Mary's power of endurance. For this woman's unconquerable pride in, unconquerable belief in James Colthurst—a pride and belief rivalling her own, yet divided from it by so frightfully different a past—was positively staggering to her reason. That roads, distinct as those leading upward to paradise, down into the abyss, should reach precisely the same end;—that she—she, Mary Crookenden, proudly clean in mind and body—that she and this poor dying prostitute should share the same longing, the same faith, the same devotion—should find their deepest joy, their deepest sorrow in love of the same man—was too bewildering a revelation of equality, of the brotherhood which, despite all our placings of higher and lower, still binds human beings together with bonds stronger than class or creed, stronger than vice and virtue, strong as life and death itself. Mary felt she must go, escape, must be by herself, silent, alone with the sad sweet music of the great Earth-Mother out in the wind and the wet, or she would have no power left to face what remained yet to be done of this strange day's work.

She rose from her knees, but the sick woman perceiving her intention, caught feebly at a fold of her dress. .

'You'm coming to see me again ? ' she gasped. 'The others is always on about Jim and his wickedness till I'm fairly mazed with their clack. You'm the only one as know, as comprehend. And then you're very good to look at, like the sun, shining and lighting up this poor place. God bless you ; I never thought to live to say that.'

And so Colthurst's letter was answered. Not telling him his love would return ; not bidding him seek his love. But bidding him hasten, put aside work, put aside anger and vengeance, forget past injuries, past offences, journey down to Beera Mills and comfort Jenny Parris as she lay on her death-bed.

CHAPTER V.

THE last of the tan-sailed herring-boats had rounded the
pier-head and sailed out into the wide bosom of the Bay, and
the night—tranquil, mild, starlit—had closed down upon
the woods and sea and the little white-walled town, when
the Rector and James Colthurst crossed the silent Square
and went up the steps leading on to the narrow, cobble-
paved platform before William Parris's cottage at the edge
of the cliff.   The rush of the stream in the gulley answered
the beat of the surf on the beach as it had done any night
there many hundred years.   The air was still, sound
carried.   Now and again the voices of the fishermen,
calling to one another as they shot the herring-nets, came
from far across the great plain of water, weird in effect,
wild as the cry of beings of another age and race.

Colthurst heard them with the same vividness of apprehension with which he heard and saw everything to-night.
His senses were preternaturally acute ; were flayed, so to
speak, offering a surface all quick to the lightest touch.
He divined, moreover, with a kind of naked distinctness,
what passed in the minds of those about him.   For him
the veils were withdrawn, the merciful veils which blunt
perception and so help to keep us sane.   To all those who
are really alive, saint, sage, artist alike, each on their
several lines, this condition is common at moments.   It
may be enchanting.   It may be hideous.   Perilous it

must always be ; for it oversteps the workable limits of human powers. In it the spirit breaks bounds, ceases to be conditioned, gets quite too close to the essence of things for personal safety. And so, in desperation, if it be a spirit finely-tempered and of noble quality, is driven to take refuge in the prayer, in which fortitude and sanity grapple an immense terror of ruin and eternal failure— the prayer ' let me not be confounded.'

And now as Colthurst stood before the old, red-cob cottage overlooking the sleeping village, fatalist though he was, that prayer rose to his lips. For the place was thick with memories, and memories are precious bad company. If evil memories, wholly bad. If sweet memories, bad company still; since what they speak of is gone and lost to us, useful only for the further furnishing of that House of Regrets, for which in youth we bake the bricks, of which in manhood we build the walls, wherein, in old age, we live. And so Colthurst paused a little, to steady himself and fight down the fear of confusion that haunted him, glancing in that rapid, quietly violent way of his, at the great dark V of the hillsides meeting in the bottom of the gulley immediately below—at the vast pallid expanse of the sea—at the overarching dome of sky, a shade darker than the sea, a shade lighter than the land, a web of fine mist drawn across it tempering the radiance of innumerable stars. Lastly he glanced at the light in the cottage window, just above him, up under the thatch.

Inside the cottage, awaiting him were realities more searching, after all, than any memories. Colthurst walked on to the far end of the platform, guarded by a broken paling, and looked down on to the beach some fifty feet beneath. He must give himself a trifle more time; he could not trust himself to meet those realities just yet.

For the light in the window symbolized that which had marred his career, crossed his high ambitions, drained away his strength like a running sore all these last eleven years. He had struggled against it, concealed it, defied the pain of it; made himself a name, a position, something approaching a fortune even, in spite of it. For the James Colthurst of to-day and the James Colthurst who had sat on the sea wall there below eleven years back were two very different men. Yet the symbol remained a true one, representing a constant quantity in his thought, a constant impediment to his freedom of action. And now the last scene of the long tragedy the symbol stood for was to be played out; to be played out, complicated by the—to him—profoundly ironical fact, that the honour and delight of his life had turned advocate for the disgrace of his life—Mary Crookenden turned advocate for Jenny Parris.

And as he stood looking down at the dimly seen beach thinking of all this, trying to overcome the bitterness it raised in him, he recalled, somehow, with singular distinctness that old boyish dream of his—of falling, falling everlastingly through space from off the edge of Saturn's luminous ring; recalled the strange hallucination which had overtaken him, here, the night of Jenny's birthday party— the day he first saw Mary Crookenden; recalled the high staircase window of the Connop School, the asphalt pavement, the chirping, impudently observant sparrows. And then the dark boulder-strewn beach seemed to call aloud to him, above the boom of its slow breaking waves and the grate of its pebbles, of rest and of emancipation—to call not as tempting him, but as promising that endurance should not fail or go unrewarded. And somehow that grim promise was very grateful to Colthurst. Sent him back to Kent Crookenden—who waited a few paces off digging the point of his walking-stick into the mould between the up-standing cobbles—braced and steadied. Let the realities be what they might he dared meet them, since behind them all, be they never so confounding, he caught sight of the form of the great deliverer, the great peace-maker, the friend to be counted on, who never fails any one of us— Death, ' delicate death.'

'I am quite ready now, Mr. Crookenden,' he said. ' Let us go in.'

The gloomy cottage kitchen, long and low as the cabin of a vessel. A heavy, fusty odour of lumber, old nets, disused lobster-pots, the accumulated dust and rubbish of many years of none too dainty house-keeping. Miss Crookenden's mulatto nurse, her swarthy profile and gay-coloured turban-like cap catching the light as she bent down tending the fire. Then the little cramped, turning staircase—the steps of it crumbling from dry-rot—which creaked complainingly beneath Colthurst's rapid tread. The open stair-head where Bill Parris slept, divided from the inner room by a thin wooden partition.—Dot slept there to-night, and the child started and turned in her sleep as he passed her.—The wooden partition is cut off straight along the top, leaving a vacant space of some two feet in the middle under the ridge beam of the roof. The door has no lintel to it, and its big wooden latch is lifted by a knotted string from without. Colthurst, alas, had lifted that latch before now ; knew the passing resistance it offered when swelled, as to-night, by recent damp ; knew the groan of the rusty hinges, as with its yielding the door swung back.

And then the room within.—For an instant all reeling together, every object in it ringed round by half the colours of the prism, then straightening back into place again, and presenting a picture of every smallest accessory of which he was vividly sensible.—The downward sweep of the raftered roof to the low side walls from off which the paper peeled in mouldy strips. The un-curtained window, directly before him in the triangle of the gable. On the right the large low bed with its unsightly sawn-off posts at the four corners. And to-night over and around that bed, and thrown up on to the raftered roof by the candle set on the sea-chest under the window, women's shadows, shifting, crossing one another, oddly deformed and distorted. And Colthurst, in his present condition of clairvoyance, forced to see those women with unsparing clearness of vision, to comprehend the relation of each to her companions, and, still worse, her relation to himself—to comprehend it in the full breadth of its incongruity, in its glaring divergence from the ordinary lines of social intercourse, in the dislocating moral problems it involved.

First—because of least consequence—Mrs. Kingdon, William Parris's sister, mother of Jenny's old sweetheart. Colthurst remembered her perfectly, had never liked her, did not like her now. A decent, dismal person, with a worried forehead and eyes at once sly and devout. A person of many trials richly enjoyed. She was engaged— Colthurst knew it, and it irritated him exquisitely—in enjoying the present trial to the uttermost, as she sat by the bedside, in black gown and all-round linen apron, with her little air of conscious forgiveness of many injuries received, wiping the moisture from Jenny's forehead or her parted lips.

Then Jenny herself—lying half over on her right side, the form of her body from shoulder to foot plainly outlined beneath the thin bed-clothes and old patch-work quilt. Her hair drawn away from her face and the nape of her neck, in a dark tangled mass, across the crumpled pillow. Her breath coming irregularly in panting, weasing sobs. Jenny—he knew that, too—stronger here on her sick bed to affect his future, nullify his dearest hopes, than she had ever been in health. And if Jenny dying was thus strong, what might not be the strength of Jenny dead? Only by a tremendous exercise of will could Colthurst check his thought, hold under his imagination, refuse to look ahead. But he checked it, held it under; for very sufficient to the present hour was the evil thereof.

And lastly, seen as across some wide blank space, inaccessible, far removed, Mary Crookenden, a strange inmate of this poverty-stricken place. Her back was towards the candle as she stood by Mrs. Kingdon, shaking out the folds of a clean, soft towel. And to Colthurst it seemed that a sort of greyness covered her, making her figure much less positive and tangible, than the crooked shadow thrown up on to the raftered roof. And as he came forward to the foot of the bed he saw her eyes close, saw her lay hold of the top of the sawn-off bed-post, knew that for the moment she suffered actual physical pain.—Ah! these realities were much worse than memories, no doubt about that.—And seeing, knowing all this, he sickened with an agony of remorse for the bitterness of the experience which his love of her, her love of him, was bringing her. His letter of three days ago appeared to him an enormity of egotism. He ought to have accepted her first recoil from him, after learning the fact of Jenny and Dot's existence. The subsequent appeal he had made to her was weak, unworthy, hysterical. Truly loving her, he ought to have let her go once and for all, go while the freshness of disgust and anger were upon her, and so saved her this present grief. It was not Jenny lying there dying whom he hated now, not Jenny whose doings were unforgiveable, but his own. And Colthurst hated himself, hated himself with an absorbing blackness of hatred for the way in which—as it seemed to him—he had dragged this beautiful woman down to his own low level; doing, in his unpardonable selfishness, the very thing which but a few months back he had scorned to contemplate—scorching not her feet only, but, as he feared, the very soul of her in the flames of his private hell.

Then indeed he did come very near being confounded. For even death, unless death meant extinction, offered, so he thought, but doubtful refuge; since while consciousness remained, it seemed to him the face of Mary Crookenden, as he saw it now with the greyness of sorrow upon it, must continue that of which he remained supremely, abidingly conscious, on and on, for ever.

But the great god Love—dear Love—though we rail at him, and rightly—for the many evils he brings on our sad human race, has still his wholly excellent aspect, his wholly divine side. He is the father of many falls, of much weeping; but he is also the father of the most gracious deeds man's history, written and unwritten, has to show.

The creak of the crazy stairs under Colthurst's tread, the

suck of the lifting latch, momentary oblivion of the truth during which her spirit had leapt up instinctively to greet him, were cruel to Mary Crookenden as the first incision of the surgeon's knife cutting down into the quivering, shrinking flesh. But now as Colthurst looked full at her, an anguish of humiliation in his eyes, Mary lost sense of her own pain in the depth of her realization of his. By the quickened insight Love gives, comprehended and, in as far as might be, answered that prayer of his against being confounded; met his eyes fearlessly, with a certain stately courage; even dared smile, gravely sweet. She spoke too, simply and to the point; trying in fine self-abnegation to turn the current of his thoughts away from herself, towards the practical matter of Jenny's piteous state.

'You are here just in time,' she said, quietly. 'We were almost afraid you might be too late. There has been another attack of hemorrhage, and it has left her very weak. But she will rally, I think. She will know you; only we must spare her any shock. We had better stay till she moves before we tell her you have come.'

And thereupon Mrs. Kingdon, a little jealous of her sick-room supremacy, elected to intervene, bringing down sentiment with a run, as you may say, from the heights of somewhat extensive tragedy to the lowlands of dismal, domestic snugness. For Mrs. Kingdon was one of those oddly-constituted persons—they are to be found in every West Country village—who revel in personally conducting a death They have the ritual of the ceremony at their fingers' ends. Charon himself might take lessons from them as to the most professional fashion of handling the oar while ferrying departing souls across the dark river. But from one cause and another Mrs. Kingdon found the proper ritual vexatiously difficult to carry out in the present case. Miss Crookenden, notwithstanding her gentleness, impressed her not a little. What was the reason of her interesting herself so much in Bill's poor, discreditable daughter ? For the life of her she could not make out. Her conscience, further, was extremely uneasy, although her vanity was extremely flattered, at being party to this secret visit of the common enemy, James Colthurst. What would Beera Town say when it came to know ? Mrs. Kingdon had a general sense of being unevenly yoked with unbelievers, of having, possibly, permitted herself to be made a cat's-paw of by Satan himself. She sighed loudly and repeatedly, regarding Colthurst, meanwhile, obliquely out of the corners of her eyes ; and being a person of principle, struggled to be true to her own small system, notwithstanding inherent difficulties, and to conduct her niece out of this world according to established precedent.

' I question if she will rally, Miss Crookenden,' she said, in a tone of complaint. ' And if I was so as to follow my own sense as to it, I should rouse her up a bit. For we'm bound to own there's signs of the end in plenty, and

I hold it's wicked to let any one—whatever they be—slip off without knowing they'm going.'

'I think she knows how ill she is just as well, probably better, than we do,' Mary answered.

Mrs. Kingdon sighed again, clasping her hands together upon her apron in the depression between her knees, and swaying herself to and fro from the waist.

'The heart's deceitful above all things,' she observed; 'an' desperately wicked, and Jenny's given them she belongs to a sight of trouble pretty near ever since she was born; and it 'ud be just of a piece with the rest if she was to slip off unawares without telling if she's turned to the Lord.—And her poor dear father out to sea with Steve too, and not a creature to be able to tell mun whether his only daughter's made her peace or not before she went.'

She debated inwardly how much further it might be safe to venture along the road of accredited ritual; for, though her appreciation of the feelings of others was comfortably circumscribed, Colthurst as he stood there at right angles to her, had an effect of still violence about him which made him appear a rather unknown and alarming being to invite to assist in the customary ceremonies of decease. All the more praiseworthy on her part, then, the effort to make him do his duty!

'If I was in your place, sir, I wouldn't reckon too much on any rallying,' she said. 'I'd bring it home to her as she was goin' for sure, and ask her about her state.'

In his present attitude of mind this suggestion struck Colthurst as almost devilishly ironical.

' W-would you, Mrs. Kingdon ? ' he stammered. ' Your niece has known me in a good many characters before now, I r-regret to say; but in that of father confessor she would hardly recognize me, I'm afraid. Sudden expressions of anxiety on my part, as to the state of her soul, m-might even seem to have an element of farce in them—h-here in this room—she lying on that bed.'

But, indeed, there was no need to rouse Jenny, for at the sound of his rapid whispering speech, she moved, straightened herself, and doing so caught sight of him. And her face, pinched and disfigured by sharp phy- sical distress, softened, lighted up, grew young. By a strong effort she raised herself on both elbows, while her hair fell dark about her shoulders ; and she laughed, actually laughed from joy at seeing him, laughed out. Then would have spoken—welcomed, thanked, praised, blessed him in her old hopelessly-hopeful fashion; but a term is set to laughter as to all else, and for Jenny that term was already fully reached. For her, the days of laughter were spent and over ; and so, rightly under- stood, this last laugh was but another added to the long list of her irremediable mistakes. It sent the blood welling up from her lacerated lungs, flowing down from her poor laughing mouth over the bosom of her night-gown on to the sheet.

'Lord a' mercy—'tis the end for certain sure,' Mrs. Kingdon cried.

And Mary Crookenden cried out, too. She could not prevent herself, the sight was too heart-rending. Then, compelled by a very storm of pity, murmuring incoherent words of comfort such as one murmurs over a child that is hurt, she bent over Jenny trying to sop it up with the towel and hide this horror of blood.

But Colthurst took the towel from her, put her at once fiercely yet tenderly aside. For that Mary Crookenden's person, or, indeed, the hem·of her garment, should come to be stained by that red tide, seemed to him the culminating grossness, indignity, disgrace, of the relation of these two women to himself.

'N-no,' he stammered, 'no, you can't, you mustn't d-do that. It passes the limits. It is my b-business, Mary, mine only—not yours.'

And then, while Mrs. Kingdon laid Jenny back upon the pillows, Colthurst, taking the bit of sponge and the little, cracked, brownish-white pudding basin of tepid water from off the chair by the head of the bed, knelt down beside her. Set his teeth hard, and in that deft, unerring fashion of his, washed her lips, chin, and throat, turned back the neck of her night-dress in front to hide that ugly soil, helped to administer such remedies as were to be had.

And for a while Mary Crookenden watched, but she could not watch for very long. Her eyebrows drew together, and the chill pride came back into her bearing. Pity gave place to an irresistible uprush of personal feeling, even of class feeling. The natural woman in Mary was affected by jealousy and resentment; the fine lady in her by social prejudice, by dainty disdain. For it was almost intolerable to her to see Colthurst minister thus to his former mistress; to see the hands she loved and in the consummate skill of which she gloried—the hands that had painted famous pictures—the hands whose touch had wakened in her knowledge of the splendour of living for those who dare sing the 'Song of the Open Road'—to see these hands busied in repulsive, menial, sick-room offices, holding a little cracked pudding basin, wringing out a bloody sponge. The girl turned away with a lift of her fair head and a rustle of silk-lined skirts over the uneven floor, pushed the small casement window wider open, looked out, deeply stirred, deeply angered, into the mild autumn night. For at Colthurst she dared not look any longer, lest feeling should master self-control, lest she should call out to him haughtily and command him to stop. And as she breathed the sweet night-air, heard the babble of the stream in the gulley, the roar of the slow breaking waves and the hiss of the surf

on the beach, Mary repented for the moment, of her own
self-abnegation. Why had she yielded to the sick woman's
entreaty, why had she bidden him come? To her it
appeared that she had been guilty of the folly of being
righteous over much.

And Colthurst noted her every movement; read, plainly,
as though it was set down in very big print, what she felt ;
knew that the crisis he had warded off so many times, the
decision which he had so often eluded, was upon him,
relentless, absolutely unavoidable at last. With Mary's
change of attitude Colthurst's had, in a measure, changed
also. He no longer feared being confounded, no longer
was aware of self-abasement. The pace was growing to
hot for all that. He could not reflect, he could only act.
And on his action during the next couple of hours—for
the bleeding had nearly ceased, the end would not be yet
—depended all his future. He foresaw that action must
determine, irrevocably for this life, to which he belonged,
which woman conquered, won, owned him—Jenny Parris,
his fellow-sinner, his comrade of evil days, peasant, model,
harlot—or Mary Crookenden, beautiful, spotlessly pure,
rich too in the good things of this world, the woman
whom he supremely honoured and loved.

Colthurst set his teeth harder ; but he finished squeezing
out the sponge, arranging the neck of the night-gown,
folding under the stained corner of the sheet, before he rose
and went back to his former station at the foot of the bed.

And Jenny, meanwhile, was unconscious of the drama being played out around her. For though the hemorrhage ceased, the bitterness of death had come upon her, following hard on that last laugh; and even when death wears a friendly aspect, that bitterness is often very great. For the soul could not easily free itself from that shapely, well-fashioned body of hers. It struggled to get loose, but the flesh held it back; and Jenny groped with her hands on the bed-clothes, her eyes staring half open as at some sight of unearthly terror,—a rattling now and again in her throat, too, between the panting, choking breaths.

The last sound was new to Mary Crookenden; and it was very ghastly. She began to listen for it; and each time it came she sickened and shuddered. She lost her count of time, as she listened; minutes seemed lengthened into hours; and that dreadful sound seemed to grow louder at each recurrence, louder than the rush of the stream, louder than the beat of the sea on the rocky beach. At length she could bear it no longer. She turned round, met Colthurst's eyes for an instant, looked away from him to the bed, came forward across the narrow space; and hearing that sound, seeing, in the flickering candle-light, those groping, searching, clutching fingers, cried, half imperiously, half imploringly, to Sarah Jane Kingdon :—

'Ah! do something, do something to help her. It is cruel, heartless, to stand by seeing her misery and doing nothing to lessen it.'

'My dear Miss, she's past help from such as us,' the
elder woman answered, in the tone of one very wrong-
fully accused. ''Tis the Almighty's ruling some should
die hard, and it's not for us to question but what all's
according to mercy. I've seen worse passings than this, so
that's not what makes me fret. What troubles me is she's
not spoke up and told if she reckons she's made her peace.'

Mrs. Kingdon shook her head and sighed heavily. Unevenly yoked with unbelievers or not, she was resolved
to bear testimony, to uphold disregarded ritual.

' We'm bound to take all that's laid upon us,' she continued. 'But 'tis no end terrifying to the mourners when
they don't know if they'm free to think comforting thoughts
of them they've lost. And her poor, dear father out to sea
and all.'

She concluded with a reproachful, sidelong glance in
the direction of Colthurst.

But to the pious woman's strictures he was, just then,
quite indifferent, for Mary, after momentarily watching
those sadly groping fingers again, turned to him, her
lips trembling with emotion, an agony of sorrow, of
relenting, of unstinted compassion in her face. She put
up her hands, pressed them against her chest to keep
down the dry sobs which almost stifled her.

' Then you must do something,' she said, her grave
voice all broken. 'You must help her, comfort her—oh !
you must—it's so dreadful to leave her all alone with her

suffering like this. And I—I won't see—I won't look—
I'll turn my back.'

And so the crisis was upon James Colthurst; the choice
placed right there before him, immediate, final. And he
knew that it was a real choice. He was free to take either
one and reject the other, nothing compelling him thereto
but his own will. The balance hung even. He was free
to throw the weight into either scale, as he pleased, that
should make it dip.

For that piteous appeal of Mary Crookenden's, the
childlike simplicity of the phrases in which she couched
it, proved to him beyond all question that her love was
intact still. Still she was his in heart. The cruel experiences of the last week had not really alienated her. Still
all his dearest, highest hopes might be fulfilled, still he
might have her as bride and wife.—The thing was as easy
—well, as easy as lying. He had only to repudiate Jenny's
moral claim on him, now at the eleventh hour, when
he had so immensely much to gain, she but the doubt-
fulest measure of good to lose by such repudiation. He
had only to echo Mrs. Kingdon's statement and declare
her beyond the reach of human help.—And after all—for
Colthurst reasoned the matter out with his usual singular
clear-headedness in presence of a searching situation—what
positive assurance had he that she was not actually beyond
the reach of such help ? How could he be certain that
now, *in extremis*, the mists of death confusing every sense,

the hands of death slowly, painfully, yet surely drawing apart and disentangling soul from body, Jenny remained capable of receiving consolation from any degree of tenderness, either of word or caress, which he—Colthurst—might lavish upon her ? Might not his labour be all in vain ? Was it not little short of insane to contemplate bartering the joy of fruitful, honourable years stretching ahead, against this very questionable chance of succouring, solacing, easing the last hours of unruly, impossible Jenny Parris ?

And then he put the case to himself from Mary Crookenden's standpoint. He perceived that she was sadly wrought upon, tired, her calm courage nearly or quite exhausted. What right had he to try her further, expose her to more of this wretchedness ? If duties were about, wasn't it a plain enough duty to take her away from this miserable scene, and place her—where of right she belonged—far from these sordid, incongruous circumstances ? To-morrow Colthurst could trust his own clever, stammering tongue and the greatness of his love, to do all that was necessary—to soften remembrance of the events of to-night and appease any inconvenient workings of her conscience. He entertained small doubt but that he could plead his own cause so as to secure the mildest of verdicts.

Yes—still, if he pleased, Mary Crookenden was his. And knowing that, he looked at her now, standing tall and fair under the ridge-beam of the raftered roof in the centre of the old, tumble-down, comfortless cottage bed-chamber, looked at her from head to foot, letting his glance rest on every graceful line, every gracious detail, drown itself in her tearful eyes, linger upon her lips—until passion waxed hot and his dark face flushed, while her actual surroundings seemed to him to fade, to be blotted out, and her figure to stand before him, naked, in all its maidenly loveliness, white as a pearl against a sheet of white flame.

For the moment Colthurst's brain reeled. The emotional side of his nature had full sway. He was reckless, mad, drunk. Then—since thanks to persistent effort, persistent struggle, spirit in the man during these twelve months had steadily gained over matter—then suddenly a great shame covered him. For it was not, surely, according to this gross pattern his love for Mary Crookenden had been conceived, brought forth, reached maturity? Appetite, so far, had never got the better of chivalrous reverence even in a glance, hardly—and that is saying a very great deal, if said truthfully—hardly in a thought, since the opening day of term at the Connop School, when he had first found her name upon the students' list.

Colthurst put his hands over his eyes to shut out the vision, bowed his head.

A silence, broken only by the laboured breathing of the dying woman. By the sanctimonious sighings of Mrs. Sarah Jane Kingdon. And—in singular contrast to these

last—the solemn voice of the sea lamenting along the coast ;
but lamenting as brave souls alone know how to lament
for the mysterious sorrow that lies at the roots of being—
acquiescent, without admixture of any sentimental self-pity,
sternly faithful in the fulfilment of their appointed work.

And that solemn voice brought good counsel.   When
Colthurst looked up he was sane.   He had laid hold of
the meaning of those tremendous sayings concerning the
plucking out of the right eye, the cutting off of the right
hand and the right foot; and having laid hold of it, had
made his choice—convinced that choice was best not only
for himself but for the woman he worshipped—had determined absolutely into which scale to drop the weight.

'Very well,' he said, quietly, ' so b-be it.   I will help her,
that is, in as far as I can.   B-but a man cannot serve two
m-masters.'

He paused, for his stammer threatened to become
ungovernable.

'Therefore farewell,' he went on, 'farewell, Mary, my
b-beloved.—And now go, in God's name, my dearest, go.
For to have you waiting and watching here while I do and
say what must pain, must almost insult you, what must
desecrate, what may render abhorrent to you the thought
of the love you have given me—t-that would be too much.
—G-go, while you can still pardon me for all the evil with
which through me you have become acquainted; while
you can still pardon the immensity of my self-seeking in

approaching you, asking you to marry me, asking you to let me mingle the foul stream of my life with the clear stream of yours. Asking you—for, God forgive me,' Colthurst broke out fiercely, ' as I see it all now it comes to nothing less than that, asking you to pay for my adoration by becoming, under the specious title of wife, the last, choicest, most precious, most costly offering I can make to my own desire.'

So far he had looked down at the uneven, worm-eaten boards while he spoke; now he raised his eyes to the girl's face.

' D-don't misunderstand me,' he said quickly. ' I don't want to discredit marriage to you and make you think slightingly of it. To the pure all things are pure. And there are men as well as women to whom marriage is pure, honourable, altogether wholesome and cleanly.'—He glanced away at the low wide bed.—'B-but I am not among them. And therefore to me it would be the last refinement of self-indulgence.'

He paused a moment, and then looked at Mary Crookenden once more, with a serenity which had a certain grandeur in it.

' And so go, my beloved,' he said very gently—' go, knowing that if souls can be saved you have done much to save mine—that if there is, as Christ preached, a life beyond this wherein man is at rest, rid for ever of the curse and burden, the fret and torment of sex, then you have done much to win that life for me by your love and your suffering. And so go, knowing that you have brought me nothing but good. Go, before I do anything further to pain you, before your love, as well as my poor discarded mistress, Jenny Parris, comes nearer lying dead.'

Colthurst moved forward, would have passed her, going round to the side of the bed. But Mary stopped him. She could not speak. But she put her hands on his shoulders, drew him towards her, kissed him on the mouth, —a kiss of renunciation, yet of faith, of strong encouragement and help. Then she let her arms drop at her sides, and with her face set like a flint, turned and went.

'Fay, who ever heard and saw the like of that?' Mrs Kingdon gasped, greatly scandalized, under her breath.

Colthurst walked straight on to the head of the bed. Sat down sideways against the sawn-off post, his back somewhat bent to avoid the low sweep of the raftered roof. He put his arms round Jenny, raised her softly, carefully, till her head rested on his shoulder where Mary's hand had rested but a few seconds ago.

'Jenny,' he stammered, 'Jenny, poor, loyal soul, come back, and whether you've made your p-peace in higher quarters or not, at least let me make my peace with you before we too part.'

CHAPTER VI.

ONLY in myth and legend do rods turn into roses. In everyday life they sternly and persistently, alas! remain rods. So it certainly appeared to Colthurst, as he leaned on the rickety paling, guarding the cobble-paved platform before William Parris' cottage, in the chill of the autumn morning, and looked across Yeomouth Bay, to where, behind the swelling uplands of the distant moor, the dawn grew and spread—primrose, saffron, scarlet, crossed by long wisps of smoke-coloured cloud, fine as a woman's hair. Over the leaden grey plain of water the herring-fleet slowly fared homeward; all save one boat, which, some half-hour ahead of the rest, was already taking up its moorings within the shelter of the sickle-shaped pier.

Mary Crookenden had gone from him. Gone, as we know, with a kiss sacred and sweet; and with her going Colthurst's gracious vision of wedded-love had fled back through the gate of dreams from whence at first it came. And Jenny Parris had gone too. Gone with a blessing, which went far to cancel the old bad score. Gone along the shadowy, silent way which leads, so some tell us, to a land where the most lovely of dreams—with a difference—come true. And now he waited till Mrs. Kingdon should have dressed Dot, and packed the child's scanty wardrobe, and made her ready to start home with him to

London, the gas, and glitter, and smoke, and stir of which she loved.

Colthurst's will was firm. His choice had been reasoned, voluntary, deliberate, final. He accepted the consequences of it unreservedly. But it would be absurd to pretend that he felt very elate. Rods were not changed to roses ; and the saying that virtue is its own reward, rightly understood, is a hard saying, not without an element of cynicism in it. No great wonder, therefore, that the future looked somewhat purposeless to him, neutral-tinted, dull and leaden as the sea spread out before him, whose furrowed surface the fair colours of the dawn as yet failed to touch. For it is no joke, depend upon it, for any child of Adam honestly, and in serious earnest, to turn monk. To extirpate 'the eternal feminine' and all that term stands to cover—its pretty minor joys and tender distresses, its merriment, its charming follies, its delightful fertility in small solacements, its inspiring revelations of unselfishness and high courage; as well as its violences, vanities, cruelties, numberless seductions, numberless delusions, unblushing lies and lusts. And yet, as Colthurst perceived—perceived with the same unsparing clearness of vision which had pursued him all that night—for a nature like his, half measures were intellectually and morally impossible. *Le mieux est l'ennemi du bien;* and to rid himself of the evil it was necessary for him also to cast away the good.

What, then, practically was left to live for ? An

idea and a fact. Art on the one hand, Dot on the other.

About the first he felt easy enough. For Art, as he reasoned, like Religion—like all the greatest ideas vouchsafed to us—lives by sacrifice, draws her vitality from the life-blood of her votaries. To secure her fulness of being and of splendour you can hardly—within the limits of sanity—sacrifice too much. She cares not a rush about the domestic happiness or material prosperity of those who devote themselves to her service. Rather does she drive them out into the wilderness, far from the common haunts of common, householding, money-making, uxorious, philoprogenitive man ; and there reveal her secrets in solitude, thirst,. and hunger, amid bare rock and burning sand. And so, telling himself this, as to coming pictures, Colthurst's mind was at rest. The extirpation of the eternal feminine, he fancied, would rather help than hinder alike their production and their intrinsic worth.

And on the other hand Dot.—Ah ! Dot presented something of a problem, for Colthurst held himself to be a strange sort of nursing mother for a very clever and rather naughty small girl. He permitted himself no sentimental, Sunday-school book illusions regarding the child and his relation to her. He foresaw collisions, embarrassments, practical difficulties in profusion. But they did not affect him much. Colthurst, in his present humour, accepted these consequences of his choice along with the rest.

'If I can only hold out,' he said to himself as he watched the widening dawn and the nearing herring-boats. 'That's all which really signifies. The truth is sad, incomparably sad. I always knew that. And to go on loving it, not flinching from it for all its sadness through years—I am in brutally good health now, so the years will probably be many— well, it will be a tough enough piece of work. Yet it is worth while,' he added. 'I'm sure I don't know why--but that it is worth while, I don't doubt. And so the one thing which signifies is to be able to hold out, decently, without whimpering or shirking, or making a show of one's sores, until death comes, at last, to close the account.'

Just then the rim of the sun's disc cleared the swelling uplands of the distant moors, sending widening rays of light flashing up to the zenith, changing the smoke-coloured cloud to flame, making a path of glory across the waters of the Bay. A glad morning wind arose, and rushed down the valley from landward. And along with the wind, so it seemed to Colthurst, a Presence, at once benign and awful, swept by him, making the frail paling quiver under his hand, and the harsh grasses and withered sea-pinks rooted in the cliff side whisper and shudder oddly as it passed.

Instinctively he turned to look up at the window of the bed-chamber where Jenny's corpse lay, the window in the gable up under the thatch. And turning, found Jenny's father, William Parris, within a couple of yards of him—a savage yet majestic figure, in his rough fishing clothes, his blue eyes wild, the salt rime frosting his beard and snarling mouth.

'Who be you?' he cried. 'What be doin' here?'— Then, in obedience to the fixed idea which possessed him, he broke out inconsequently :—

'Woe to the fulish virgins, woe to the rebellious daughters, and to them what leads mun captive wi' lying words.'

'Woe enough,' Colthurst thought, 'God knows.'

But when he tried to answer, to quiet the man, to tell him that with Jenny, at all events, it was well, since, forgiving and forgiven, she had entered into rest, once again Colthurst's tongue played him false. He was very tired. He stammered, stammered badly, could not articulate a single intelligible sentence. Stood dumb, in all the pathos of utter incapacity either of explanation or self-justification, as far as speech went—his eloquence useless, his repentance, his sacrifice, his expiation doomed to silence, since his body thus in his extremity had turned traitor to his brain.

Exactly what took place, neither Stephen Kingdon, who followed close behind, nor Kent Crookenden, who was coming up the steps from the Square—having returned from taking his niece home to Brattleworthy—can say. Whether the old man, maddened by Colthurst's silence, actually struck him, or whether Colthurst, not choosing to defend himself, backing away from his assailant, backed too far, Steve Kingdon does not

know.   But he knows this, that as he ran up and caught
Bill Parris round the shoulders and hauled him off, the
crazy paling cracked, gave—splintering right and left like
so much matchwood, and Colthurst pitched right back
over the cliff edge.   For an instant his face caught the
sunlight, as his body turned in the air ; while with a great
shout—which rang along the coast, and out across the
tranquil Bay, and over the sleeping, white-walled town,
and up into the windings of the wooded combe—a shout
of triumph, of consummated warfare, of emancipation,
of hope—that strong soul hailed Death,—the consoler,
the restorer, ' delicate Death '—sitting waiting for him
just this side the white line of the slow-breaking waves on
the purple-grey shingle fifty feet below.

And that is why they dug two graves within the week,
side by side, in the little churchyard half-way up the
combe ; and why they flew the flags, down in Beera village,
half-mast high.

EPILOGUE.

IT is given to few to realize their ideals—to the few, not
to the many.   All the more soothing and refreshing, then,
to let thought dwell awhile upon the happy state of those
favoured few.

And to begin with, the Council of the Connop Trust
School may claim to stand among those consolatory few.

For it the days of doubt and misgiving, of sitting on the edges of official chairs, are over. It made much handsome mention of the great services rendered to the school by its late director, James Colthurst. Inserted the said mention, not without rhetorical flourishes, in the 'minutes' of its meeting; and promptly proceeded to fill the vacant post with a very safe, very innocuous, and very-much-married gentleman of conservative views and middle age. Realism and subversive tendencies have vanished from the Connop School. And Mr. Barwell has vanished also—has retired finally and permanently to the semi-detached villa and society of the gentle parrot-nosed sisters at Hampstead. Not that the incoming director wished to eject the under-master. He would gladly have retained his services. But no, Mr. Barwell could not stay—having held office under King Stork, he could not make up his mind to hold office under any King Log again. It was foolish of the good man. The work would have been light; under the new *régime* he might have drum-doodled along in the easiest possible fashion. But the spectacle of Colthurst's tremendous vitality had fascinated him; and to him the Connop School, without that spectacle, was a little too melancholy. He could not stand it.

And next, among the consolatory few, we may number that extremely pretty little person, sometime Violet Winterbotham. For several winters now, both at the Hunt Ball at Slowby and the Bachelors' Ball at Tulling-

worth, she has appeared dazzling, dimpling, most decora-
tive of dormice, in all the Aldham family diamonds.
The year after his nephew's engagement came to such a
very lame conclusion, Sir Reginald, still inconsolable for
his wife's death and in lively search of consolation, happened to meet the Winterbothams at Homburg. Lady
Sokeington, *née* Barking, says she can't conceive how any
girl can quite make up her mind to marry a man three
times as old as herself.   But adds that—'darling
Vi always was wonderfully sensible, and that it is
too delightful for words to have her settled just next
door, as you may say, in Midlandshire; and that the son
and heir is quite the trottiest of trots.   And, of course,
young Mr. Crookenden was really more than slow and
tiresome about his affair.   And then, after all, his father
was only a Bristol shopkeeper—merchant ?—oh, well it's
very much the same thing, after all—though his mother is
tidily connected ; so clearly this marriage is infinitely the
nicer of the two.   And dear Sir Reginald is more than
off his head about her ; Vi is quite *the* love of his life,
one can see that. And then there *is* something very touching
about being an old man's darling; and if Vi doesn't mind
the disparity, why really nobody else need worry about it,
at least that is what she, Lady Sokeington, thinks.'

And little Dot may be reckoned among the consolatory
few, also, for she seems to be in a fair way to attain her
ideal.   She danced, not at the Slowby Hunt Ball last

Christmas in diamonds, like young Lady Aldham, but at the Covent Garden pantomime, in the most delightfully abbreviated of skirts and the gayest of tinsel, which regarded from a certain level is every bit as useful and meritorious a proceeding. She wore wings, actually wings like a butterfly's, with great gilt-paper eyes on them. It was enchanting, heavenly. And Mr. Snell, of Shepherd's Bush, made himself a positive nuisance by the vigour of his applause in the topmost gallery. Other and more influential persons than the enthusiastic Snell remarked the little girl's performance also; with consequences, for it was evident the child, small and light-made as she is, has real talent. And so, although—as Mrs. Prust loses no opportunity of informing all whom it may or may not concern—'there is no need for the poor little mortal to work for her living, because even if she hadn't a little something of her own, which she has, she—the speaker—and Capt'n Prust have plenty enough to provide for her,' it is probable Dot will dance her way through the world; and that her name, before long, will come to figure in play-bills, and her quaint, shrewd, able, little face in photographers' windows and the pages of dramatic journals. Let no one be alarmed. Mrs. Prust will prove a capable guardian of her morals; and neither Dot's heart or head are of the same quality as her mother's. She is not of the sort who make shipwreck. She is too clever; shall we add she is not sufficiently generous-natured? For, though possibly the admission

is a dangerous one in some of its aspects, it does undeniably take a rather superb generosity to throw yourself
away according to the superabundantly reckless fashion of
poor Jenny Parris.

And mention of photographic studios suggests further
thought of Cyprian Aldham. For that gentleman's delicate, fine-featured countenance is conspicuous just now in
the large window in the Strand, from behind the plate
glass of which—set in little rows, both clothed in the full
canonicals of their respective professions—celebrated
comedians and celebrated ecclesiastics look forth side by
side, with a millennial harmony that, as one fancies, might
prove rather startling to the fathers of the Early Church.
Mr. Aldham, after some years of really admirable London
mission work, has been offered—so the *Guardian* announces
—and has accepted the newly-created Indian bishopric of
Munipur and Gowhatty. No doubt he will do laudable
service there to the Anglican Communion. As to the
future of Cyprian Aldham likewise, no fears need be
entertained.

But how about the goodly youth Lance ; is he fated to
realize his ideal or not? That is precisely what Mrs.
Crookenden would be so extremely obliged if any one would
tell her. She still regards her niece Mary from the point of
view of disapproval. But her disapproval runs on quite
other lines than the old; for it is the young lady's con-
stancy rather than her tendency towards new and surpris-

ing departures which now so greatly vexes her aunt. Is Lancelot to be kept waiting for ever? Mrs. Crookenden asks.

And Lancelot himself cannot answer that question. He only knows he cannot change. How on earth can you change when you have felt just the same ever since you can remember? And therefore perhaps—though Polly is so awfully good and kind to him and seems so willing to have him on hand to look after her and do her odd jobs, that he can't help sometimes being a little encouraged about it all—perhaps it would be wiser to make up his mind that he will always have to wait. This was what he told Lady Calmady when last he talked the matter over with her, walking up and down the broad southern terrace at Brockhurst, which overlooks the sloping paddocks where the dainty-limbed yearling fillies feed, the stately avenues of elm and lime, and the dark ridges of the fir forest. Lady Calmady spoke comfortably to him, smiling at him with her delightful smile—for she and her husband have a very true fondness for the goodly youth—telling him to wait yet a while longer and then take heart of grace.

And Mary? She has disappeared from the smart world, and from the world of art as well, for the last few years. Vague rumours of her come from distant quarters. Evershed and his wife caught a glimpse of her at Cairo. And about fifteen months later, Horatio Deland, the Thought-Reader—who is making a tour of the world to collect per-

fectly reliable information for that new and very illumina-
ting association known as the S.R.E.S.O.I. —in a letter to
Adolphus Carr, mentioned that he was almost certain it
was she whom he met in the gateway of a temple at Tokio,
one day in early summer, when the fruit-trees were all in
bloom.   Kent Crookenden has been travelling with her.
He put in a *locum tenens* at Brattleworthy—a diligent,
praiseworthy young cleric, who, it may be mentioned in
passing, calls increasingly often at Slerracombe House,
furnished with an increasing amount of interesting parochial
business, the detail of which he finds it increasingly necessary to discuss with that best of good-hearted young
women, Carrie.

Madame Jacobini remains in the little blue house in St.
George's Road.   For, as she said to Kent Crookenden :—

'I really am too old to live in my boxes, and be on view
and equal to the situation, morning, noon, and night.   A
woman who respects herself and other people's eyes will
go into retirement for a large number of hours out of every
twenty-four, if she is wise, when the grand climacteric has
come within sight.   Travelling brings out all the weak
spots in one's looks, manners, and temper.   No, thank
you, the tax on one's own vanity and one's neighbours'
forbearance is too severe.   And, moreover, Mary will be
just as well away from me.   We women are invariably too
intimate when we care for each other.   We relax each
other's tongues, under the plea of communion and sympathy,

and encourage each other to say a thousand and one things that had better be left unsaid.'

Madame Jacobini made a small grimace. Her tears were rather near the surface somehow.

'We enervate each other abominably,' she went on. 'Carry the dear child off, and keep her from me till the wound has healed a little—poor darling.'

And so, troubled by a spirit of rather cruel unrest, our proud milk-white maiden wandered away, as so many another before her has wandered, trying to cheat sorrow by change of place. Wandered through the magic East, mother of religions, mother of countless millions of human worshippers. Wandered on to tropic islands lying like jewels on the bosom of the summer sea. And on again till East turns West, and ancient civilizations gave place to civilizations that count fewer years than the others count centuries. From Asia, ripe to rottenness, to America, crude often to commonness; yet rich with the promise of the days to come, as the former is rich with the splendour of days that are past. While more than once during her wanderings, the turn of a sentence suddenly heard, the tone of a voice, a rapid gesture, a figure momentarily caught sight of on railway station, or steamer-deck, in crowded eastern bazaar or equally crowded western street, has made the girl's heart stand still, and the blood leave her lips, with the ache of longing for what has been and is not. And then the unrest, which might have seemed for a space in abeyance, has seized her

again, bidding her wander further, further yet, on her
pilgrimage after a lost good.   For that is the worst of the
wages of sin. Sinners cannot pay them all—however willing, however passionately desirous even they may be to do
so. Those wages are always paid in part, of necessity must
be, by the innocent in place of the guilty.

But, at last, in that New World, where we of the Old
World fancy hope has her dwelling—but in a part of it
touched by the pathos of payment, on a very large scale, of
certain wages of sin—it came about that Mary Crookenden,
in obedience to a simple and, on the surface of it, very
inadequate cause, began at last to overget her spirit of
unrest.

It happened thus.   Lancelot—rather incited thereto
by Lady Calmady, I believe—joined the travellers in New
York. And while there the fancy took Miss Crookenden to
journey down south and visit her mother's home.   An unknown uncle and aunt—bachelor and spinster—still live in
a portion of the large, wide-verandahed mansion, with
quaint mixture of straitened means and stately etiquette.
And there, one day, waiting under the magnolias before
the house, for Lancelot and one of the negro servants to
bring round the horses for her early ride, Mary, moved by
a sudden impulse, said to the Rector, as he stood by her
holding her whip while she fastened her gloves :—

'Tell me, Uncle Kent, what does one end by doing when
all the best is taken away from one, when life has grown

trivial, stunted, and narrow; when the sun of one's happiness is set ?'

And Kent Crookenden mused a little, letting his kindly eyes rest first on the great half-ruinous house, and then on the girl's face, white as the opening magnolia blossoms above her head.

'After a time, Polly, not at once—that would be asking too much of poor human nature—but after a time, my dear, one lights a candle called Patience, and guides one's footsteps by that.'

'Do you speak out of your own experience ?' Mary asked, gravely.

'Yes,' he said.

And then he rehearsed to her the story of a courtship which had gone forward, in this very Coudert Mansion, over thirty years ago.

'To the best of my ability I lighted that candle the day your mother told me which of the two brothers who loved her she loved best. It burnt very badly at first, Polly, did my candle—guttered, had thieves in the wick ; and meanwhile I stumbled pretty freely. But, by God's grace, it has burnt brighter as time has gone by—burns brightly enough now, as I humbly trust, to light me down the long hill of old age without any very discreditable tumbles.'

'Ah, dear Uncle Kent,' Mary exclaimed, softly.

The Rector felt for the black ribbon, and drew the little faded miniature out from its hiding-place.

'There is my romance,' he said. 'This is like her, but you are more like. And so you are very dear to me for sake's sake, as well as for your own. Try to light your candle of Patience, my Polly, in faith ; remembering that you are not alone. More than half the noblest men and women you meet carry such candles likewise.—Ah ! here come Lancelot and the horses.—Steady—are you all right ? Wait a moment, let me put your habit straight. Don't go too far and tire yourself.—Take good care of her, Lance.'

THE END.